Dear Michelle.

and fulfilling Wis
journey throu

With love & blessings,

Ann

XXX

The Ascension Prophecy

The Time is NOW!

Ann Campbell

Illustrations and map by

Maggie Kneen

Photographs by Ann Campbell

First published by Amazon, USA

Typeset by John Beaumont

To contact the author:

Facebook: The Ascension Prophecy

Email: anncampbellnexus@gmail.com

This book is dedicated to my amazing children, Rachel, Laura and Amelia, and to my beautiful grandchildren, Megan, Ryan, Oakley, Rio and James.

Foreword

Dear Reader,

This is an invitation for you to join me on an adventure of a life-time. Whether you are young or old or in-between, take heart, for you will only need a comfy chair and a child-like curiosity. There is magic, mystery and hope to be found within these pages ...

The story begins with a seemingly ordinary family, preparing for a summer holiday in S.W. France. Soon, stirrings of an otherworldly nature bring each member, children and grown-ups alike, together in a common goal. They have been chosen to assist in the clearing of old, destructive energies from beautiful and dramatic sites. They will need to set up an Energy Matrix in preparation for an extraordinary event that has been foretold. This will have momentous repercussions for the future of Mankind.

I hope that you enjoy this book and are drawn to read it again and again. May we all have the courage and commitment to look beneath the surface of our own lives, and find the truth, guidance and joy that are hidden there. Be prepared for miracles!

With love and best wishes,

Ann Campbell

Chapters

Photographs and Illustrations

The Ascension Prophecy

The Time is NOW!

Ann Campbell

MYSTERY, MAGIC & ADVENTURE ~ in the ~ LANGUEDOC-ROUSSILLON

Toulouse

Carcassonne

ARIÈGES

Mirepoix

Limoux

L'AUD

Lavalanet

Peyrepertuse

Montségur

Quéribus

Axat

St-Paul-de-
Fenouillet

Puilaurens

PYRÉNÉES

ORIENTALES

Pic du
Canigou

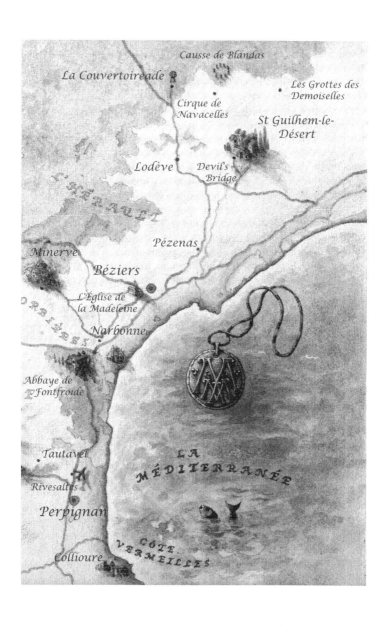

Causse de Blandas

La Couvertoirade

Les Grottes des
Demoiselles

Cirque de
Navacelles

St Guilhem-le-
Désert

Lodève

Devil's
Bridge

L'HÉRAULT

Pézenas

Minerve

Béziers

L'Église de
la Madeleine

CORBIÈRES

Narbonne

Abbaye de
Fontfroide

Tautavel

LA
MÉDITERRANÉE

Rivesaltes

Perpignan

Collioure

CÔTE
VERMEILLES

Les Remparts

Prologue

One mortal blow felled the chain-mailed giant as his helmet clattered to the ground, his undrawn sword a sceptred splint. A young woman watching from an archway darted towards him and sank down to cradle his head. He groaned as a shudder coursed upwards through his stricken body, a deep crimson rivulet oused from his trembling mouth.

"Save me, Mégane...pray for my soul..." he whispered.

She lowered her face to his and lightly kissed his cool, damp forehead, brushing the thick locks of hair from his brave face. A deep sob escaped her tightened throat and she uttered a blessing, "May God and all His angels guide you and keep you. Amen."

She felt the life-force ebb from his fallen flesh as a veil of peace moved lightly across his visage. She closed his eyelids one by one and withdrew into the shadows as darkness fell.

1

Languedoc-Roussillon Arrivals

Bella and Jean-Paul were waiting in Arrivals at *Rivesaltes* Airport. It was approaching midday when the Worthington family came into view. There were hugs and kisses on both cheeks and a real delight at seeing how much the children had grown since last Christmas.

"*Bonjour, ça va?*" asked Jean-Paul in his lilting French accent. "Have you had a good flight?"

"*Oui, ça va bien. Et toi, Oncle Jean-Paul?*" Megan, Tom and Lily replied laughingly. They were definitely going to brush up their French!

Jean-Paul gave Steve a hug and Steve kissed his sister-in-law. Then the children's aunt and uncle led the way outside into the hot summer sunshine towards their parked Renault.

Bella turned to Steve. "I thought we could stop for lunch in *Tautavel,* about half-way between here and home."

"That's a really good idea; a French meal and a glass of *Fitou* would go down a treat."

"It's a lovely little village on the banks of the *Verdouble,*" Bella continued. "It's become a major centre of prehistory. There's evidence to show that prehistoric man and animals lived in this area up to

700,000 years ago. The prehistoric hunter, *Tautavel Man*, lived on the *Roussillon* plains about 450,000 years ago."

"Wow! How do we know that?" asked Tom.

"Is there anything we can see there?" Megan added eagerly.

"Tools and human remains have been found and they can be quite accurately dated."

"There's a vast museum of European Prehistory just a little further north. We could call there after lunch," Jean-Paul suggested.

"That sounds very interesting," said Lily, trying to imagine what human beings would have looked like all those years ago.

They parked in the shade of the tiny square and ambled to the bistro, which had green metal tables set outside. They all looked at the menu. Then the children went to find *les toilettes* whilst the adults ordered aperitifs and cold *oranginas*. Steve fancied the *coq-au-vin*, Jean-Paul and Bella chose *magret du canard à la pâte*, Lily wanted an *omelette au fromage*, and Tom and Megan, *les moules-frites*. Tom had thought of ordering the *cuisses de grenouilles* but maybe frogs' legs would make Lily queasy *before* they got back into the car! She was doing quite well up to now. They all had *crème caramel* for dessert and then the grown-ups finished with a coffee.

In the square, several merchants displayed their goods; there was wine for sale, a baker's and butcher's, and a small chemist's shop. A stone obelisk stood outside the latter, which displayed a carving of the Staff of Hermes. Two coiled serpents wound their way up either side of a staff; it was the *Caduceus.*

"I've never seen one of those before," commented Lily. "What does it mean?"

"It's an ancient symbol used by the medical profession to represent balance and healing," Bella told her.

"And a similar symbol is used on the World Health Organisation flag, though it only has one serpent," Steve added.

They returned to the car and drove up to the Museum of European Prehistory. Using the latest technology and state-of-the-art scenography, everyone was taken back in time. The rooms had interactive control panels and screens giving a variety of fascinating information: from man's place in the universe to the tools used by *Tautavel Man.*

The children were totally absorbed. They asked Bella and Jean-Paul lots of questions about the *Languedoc-Roussillon* area which included the *Pyrénées Orientales*, the *Aude* and the *Hérault* regions.

Jean-Paul explained that they would be visiting these three areas in the coming weeks.

"Which part is the most interesting?" Lily asked.

"Each area has a lot of things to see and do," replied Jean-Paul, "so you'll have to tell us what you think when you've been to all three."

During the last part of the journey, Tom gazed up at the skyline and thought the light was different than at home. He caught sight of a castle, silhouetted against the bright azure sky, high on a craggy outcrop to his right.

"Hey, look at that! How many points do I get for spotting that?"

"Definitely ten!" called Jean-Paul from the front of the car.

"*Quéribus* is a Cathar Castle in the *Aude* region. We thought you'd find them interesting," said Bella.

"How do you get up there?" asked Lily.

3

"With ropes and crampons," Tom said, trying to keep his face straight.

"They look, and are, very impressive. You can follow the road up near to the top of *Quéribus*, then it's possible to walk right up to the entrance," Jean-Paul told them.

Steve gave Tom a disparaging look.

"Oh, I'd love to see what it's like inside," said Lily in a dreamy voice. "There may be towers and princesses and spells and knights."

"Oh no!" groaned Tom.

"There's lots of history connected to these castles," Megan chipped in, "so we can read up on them before our visit."

"We've got books and pamphlets on a variety of topics to do with this area. They're all in the study so you can borrow them whenever you like," said their uncle.

"Is it far now?" asked Lily. "Only I'm feeling a bit hot."

"We'll be home in ten minutes. Then you can jump into the plunge-pool," Bella reassured her.

They drove past the low sign of "*St-Paul-de-Fenouillet*"; the name being indicative of the wild fennel that grew in the region. Scattered houses of various shapes and sizes nestled in the natural folds and seams of the verdant French countryside. Streams, lanes and railway tracks collaborated in a comfortable patchwork of amenities for *les habitants*.

Jean-Paul pulled into the driveway and those nearest the doors flung them wide open. The mainly brick-built house had three storeys including the basement, part of which formed the garage.

"Let's have a quick look around then you know where you're sleeping," said Bella, leading the way.

"Then we can go out onto the terrace and you can explore the garden."

Steve and Jean-Paul unloaded the car so that it could be driven down into the cool garage. Bella went up a flight of wide, carpeted stairs to two medium-sized rooms that shared a connecting shower-room.

She turned to Megan. "Will you and Lily be all right in these?"

"Oh, yes, it's lovely up here, so light and pretty."

"Would you mind sharing with Lily just for one night, Megan, so that your Dad can have your room?"

"Of course not, Aunt Bella, I can still unpack some of my things later."

"I'll have this room, the one next to Tom's," Lily confirmed.

"Will you be alright in the room next to the bathroom, Tom?" "Yes, it looks very comfortable," he said, stepping through the doorway, "and there's a desk to put my laptop on and a telescope. I bet Dad will be using that later."

Steve worked at Jodrell Bank, the Cheshire observatory, for part of the week, and taught Astrophysics at Manchester University during the remainder.

Tom made his way over to the window. "What a huge garden!"

"Yes, it keeps us busy. I hope you and the girls will enjoy being outdoors for much of the holidays. We're so lucky with the climate here."

Tom turned to face a wall covered in a large, detailed map of France and a smaller map of the world. "It's got everything I need," Tom told Bella enthusiastically.

Bella smiled. "Uncle Jean-Paul tends to plan his trips from here if I'm hogging the study. Come down when you're ready."

Tom raced downstairs with the girls just behind him, through the dining-kitchen and out onto the terrace. Jean-Paul had made a jug of lemonade with lemons from a tree in the orchard and plenty of ice-cubes. Steve helped himself to mixed olives and Megan and Tom raided the cashew nuts while Lily sank into a deep cushion on a wicker chair, her feet swinging freely.

"How's school been this year?" Jean-Paul asked them.

"Good!" said Megan.

"I've won a few more sprinting and swimming trophies at county level so my new school won't be disappointed in the scholarship they've awarded me. I just hope I can keep the momentum going next year."

"I'm sure you will!" Bella said confidently.

"What about you, Tom?"

"Oh, I've got some good mates at school and I've enjoyed my violin and maths lessons best of all. I've been picked for the football team a couple of times which was really fantastic!"

"And Lily, how've you been getting on?" Jean-Paul asked kindly, knowing that she was not as confident as her elder siblings.

"I like my school. We've been having French lessons. And I like art and getting a part in the school play...I had to sing and everything."

"She played Mole, didn't you Lils, in an excerpt from *Toad of Toad Hall*. And she was rather good!" Tom added with a hint of pride.

"My goodness! Well done, Lily. I wish I'd been there." Bella smiled affectionately.

After downing their lemonade, the youngsters ran through the garden. Lily squatted by the pond and watched the dance of iridescent dragonflies, newts diving and skaters zig-zagging across the surface. She wished she'd got a pooter and a net. The purple buddleias were covered in exquisitely-coloured butterflies and Megan was having a closer look. Tom noted the sandy, flat area under the shade of the plane tree for playing *boules* and then jumped onto the tree-swing. Cooler wafts of air brushed past his temples; he felt free and relaxed as the swing went higher.

Nearer to the house stood a circular plunge-pool and, on the other side, a table was set up for games. Beyond all these was a half-acre orchard where Jean-Paul and Bella grew a variety of fruits including figs and olives. To the side of the house stood a greenhouse, a vegetable plot and some soft fruit trellises. They enjoyed growing as many of the fresh fruits and vegetables as they could manage, trying to keep to organic methods, even planting seeds in accordance with the phases of the moon.

Megan decided to change into her swimwear and cool off in the pool. Bella had put out lots of towels on their beds, including beach towels for outside. Lily and Tom soon joined her and there were shrieks of delight following each loud splash.

"How's Laura?" Bella was asking Steve.

Bella was five years older than her sister and had lived in France since meeting Jean-Paul Lefèvre as modern language students at the *Sorbonne*. She had been concerned for Laura after Lily's birth, when some kind of unusual experience had frightened her and sapped her energy. Her sister had never fully recovered.

"She's doing really well and she's delighted with this summer's arrangements. It's all thanks to you two. Just the thought of a few weeks to herself has given her confidence a boost. Laura wants to go to Lourdes before we join you here."

"I'm so glad to hear it, Steve."

7

"What are your travel plans then?" asked Jean-Paul.

"We're flying to Paris for a few days before going down to Biarritz and then on to Lourdes. We'll get here for the last week in August, of course, to share Megan's and Tom's birthdays."

"I can't believe they're going to be thirteen and twelve this year. And Lily's catching them up; she'll be eleven next March! Whilst you're in Paris, why not take Laura to *Boffinger's Brasserie* in the Bastille area? It's got a fantastic atmosphere, and the food is delicious," Bella suggested.

She went to make coffee while Steve and Jean-Paul sat chatting.

"How's work going?" Jean-Paul asked, knowing that Steve's job as an astrophysicist could sometimes get very intense.

"Really interesting at the moment. There's new information coming through all the time at *JBCA* and I've finished my lectures for a few months so I've got more time for my own research — and the family, of course. Have you done any stargazing lately?"

"I tend to be more occupied with the outdoor-pursuits courses at this time of year, as you know but, come the shorter days, I'll be out here."

Just after six, Jean-Paul said that he would prepare a salad to accompany the *charcuterie.* Lily wanted to help so she went with her uncle to pick some fresh ingredients. Megan set the table and Steve, Bella and Tom went for a game of *boules.*

As the colour drained from the sky, evening birdsong pierced the cooling air. Tom, his dad and uncle, strolled through the damp grass to the bottom of the garden with the telescope. The girls settled themselves in the comfortable sitting-room

8

and began to inspect Bella's large collection of crystals and fossils.

"Where have all these come from, Aunt Bella?" Megan was picking up a large and very heavy piece of amethyst.

"All over the world, really. We've been collecting them for years. The geode you're holding came from Brazil when we went there about five years ago. It's amazing to think that such beautiful crystals have grown in the dark, deep within the earth. I particularly like amethyst; it's a very soothing and healing stone and it's said to encourage spiritual development so I usually meditate here, where this piece is."

"Why do you meditate?" Lily asked.

"It's a way of relaxing, allowing the mind to become still yet alert. It sounds so simple but it does take practice. Then you start to tune into your inner world and inner wisdom."

Lily was rolling a piece of amber through her fingers as she leaned towards the shaded light of a nearby lamp.

"This is so smooth," she said, "and it's warm. I can see something inside it!"

"Yes, it's fossilised tree resin and often contains an insect or seed. What can you see?"

"It looks like a seed. What can you use amber for?"

"Amber's been used for thousands of years for healing. It's associated with the throat area and the *solar plexus*, where we sometimes feel emotions knotted up. Amber helps us to speak our own truth and purify all aspects of us: mind, body and spirit. It can also help the earth to give up her secrets," Bella told them.

"That sounds very mysterious," Megan commented.

"It's interesting to think that we're finding out about the past all the time. Artefacts are being unearthed or they simply come to the surface."

"You mean like the tools that we saw earlier, used by *Tautavel Man*...and the Staffordshire Hoard?" Megan realised.

"Yes! Exactly! Archaeologists, metal detectorists, and people just looking around on the ground, are finding exceptional things."

The girls continued to pick up and scrutinise various items.

"Jean-Paul also finds interesting things when he goes caving and climbing. He always brings them back to try to identify them. If you close your eyes and simply feel a stone you may sense something more from it. They all have different energy or vibrations."

L'Hermitage de St Antoine

2

L'Hermitage de St Antoine

On Tuesday morning it was decided that the family would explore the local area, beginning with a visit to the *Gorge de Galamus*. Here, St Anthony's Hermitage was sited. Steve was going to join his children on the trip and then would be catching a flight home late-afternoon.

It was a warm, sunny morning and everyone was wearing shorts; but Bella had said they needed sweaters too because there was a strong wind-chill factor in the gorge.

They piled into the waiting car and drove the short distance, past the railway station, turning right onto the D7 which climbed steeply towards the gorge.

"I sometimes bring students canoeing through here," Jean-Paul told the children. "It's very impressive, as you'll see when we park up."

"How will we reach the hermitage?" asked Lily.

"On a zip-wire!" Tom answered breezily.

"Well you can go first!" said Megan.

"Actually, although it looks quite daunting from the car park, there's a footpath to the cave," Bella reassured Lily.

"And there's a refreshments' kiosk in the car park."

"You can't actually see the river until we leave the car but driving through the sheer, overhanging rock is very atmospheric," said their uncle. "It's very narrow in parts, so narrow you could get stuck. But we haven't yet, have we Bella?" he added, winking.

Jean-Paul parked and the children jumped out and ran to look over the edge where a ribbon of glistening blue water could be seen. The gorge formed a deep cleft in the rock and the hermitage looked as if it was hanging by an invisible thread. The children were very excited to get onto the narrow ledge that hugged the side of the gorge. Tom led the way along the compacted, bare earth that dipped in the middle. The rhythm of their feet seemed to mark time like centurians, though the route was starkly different.

As they approached the hermitage, Tom darted into a stone orifice as if grabbed by some unseen hand. It took a few moments for his eyes to adjust to the gloom; points of light flickered into his awareness from triangular niches. He peered through a milky haze and his heart banged in his chest. His palms became uncomfortably clammy even as a chill swept over his shoulders. Tom wiped his hands down the sides of his shorts and cool drops of sweat ran down the back of his neck.

Tom stumbled into a wooden structure. He felt the gnarls and gaping cracks with his hands, which spread outwards as far as he could reach. His feet were propped apart by what felt like a sturdy post. Without any warning, it lurched backwards! He found himself spread-eagled along what he assumed to be a crucifix, facing and supported by its extended beams.

The wood itself seemed to be pulsating in time with his heartbeat and a warm glow began to radiate from the centre of his chest. He heard the words, *I am with you.*

"Who's there?" Tom called.

Tom didn't know what was happening. He clambered down onto the uneven stone floor and turned to see streams of light entering the cave. His heartbeat began to settle and instead of being afraid, he felt strangely comforted.

He saw the faces of Megan and Lily appear in the opening.

"There you are! We thought you'd got lost!" Megan exclaimed. "Are you all right Tom?" Lily asked, making her way towards him. "I've been worried about you."

"Yes, I'm all right *now.*"

"We've just bought some tapers from the kiosk out there, and some cards, and look at these — one's yours." Lily held out her hand where two gleaming stones nestled.

"Pick one," she told him.

He chose the smooth, green stone with the swirls of cream shot through it and left the pale pink one for Lily.

"That's aventurine; maybe it gives courage to adventurers," Megan joked.

Tom hoped so.

"I chose amber. Aunt Bella says it's good for the memory." Megan took it out of her pocket to show him.

Meanwhile, Lily went over to a shallow ledge to light her tapers. "Just imagine living here by yourself, for years and years like St Anthony did."

"He was a brave man for sure," responded Tom, remembering his earlier experience and shuddering a little.

"I wonder if his prayers were answered?"

"Let's hope so. People like him are very special and pray for the whole world," Megan told them.

Steve followed the path round and went up a few steps until he came to a statue. He saw three figures: Christ was raised at the back as if ascending into heaven; a woman was sitting on the right, in the foreground — she was looking into a mirror but was wearing a blindfold; a second woman was standing to the left, gazing up at Christ.

Steve pondered the meaning of this scene.

Christ et L'Humanité

The woman looking at Christ seemed captivated by what she saw and filled with hope. The other woman appeared to have no hope. In fact, she was blind to it, ensnared in the world. Steve felt a sensation like pins and needles spread downwards from his head. In some mysterious way, his faith in God had come to life in that moment, become real.

They all met up a while later and followed the path to a flight of steps that led onto the road.

"This is the easier way back," said Bella, "but we wanted you all to experience the magical route first."

"It *is* magical. It looked so inaccessible but we all got there, didn't we? Did you enjoy that, Lily?" Megan asked her.

"Oh yes! And did you feel the peace inside the hermitage, Daddy?"

"Yes I did, Lily."

The steep, narrow road necessitated a single file until they reached the car park, where they had an ice cream treat.

In the afternoon, Jean-Paul drove Steve to the airport. The children had said their goodbyes and were enjoying the outdoors. Tom and Megan played table tennis whilst Lily collected a mixture of flowers to display on the outside table. When Bella had made some refreshments, she told them that she and Jean-Paul had a surprise for them. They tried to guess what it was, without success. Bella resisted the temptation to tell them until her husband got home.

Waiting in the basement were three brand new bikes and three cycling helmets. Later that day, when it was a bit cooler, they would all cycle into the village. The children would be elated! In the past they'd had second-hand ones. Now they all had stylish frames and, hopefully, some freedom to explore the locality.

That evening, as Jean-Paul prepared a meal, Lily asked her uncle,

"Do you always cook dinner?"

"Not always, but often. My parents used to own a small bistro in Paris. I learned a lot about the business and used to help out when I was a student there. I really enjoy cooking."

"I do too," she confided. "I like making up recipes and adding herbs. I'll help you if you like."

"Oh thank you, Lily. You can make something for us another day if you want to."

Bella and the older children set the table outside. They were discussing what they were going to do later in the week.

"The weather's so lovely, I hope we can go to the beach one day," Megan suggested.

"Of course we can. The coast is only forty kilometres away."

"I can't wait to go to a castle. Our friend, Andrew, was telling me more about the *Knights Templar* before we came away. Have you ever met Andy, Aunt Bella?"

"No, I don't think I have. How old is he?"

"He's twenty. You know Gill, our baby-sitter, well he's Gill's boyfriend and lives in Alderley Edge. In September, he'll be in his third year at Manchester Uni where he's doing physics and electronics. He bumps into Dad sometimes."

"Andrew sounds very bright! Anyway, this area is renowned for those knights, Tom, so we'll definitely visit some castles."

Just then, Jean-Paul called out to tell them that dinner was ready. The bike-ride had given them all a good appetite.

3

The Illusion of Time

Over breakfast on the terrace they planned the day's outing. "It's a perfect day to visit the beach and do some sight-seeing in *Collioure,*" Jean-Paul announced, showing them a detailed map. "What do you think?"

Megan and Tom wanted to visit the Knights Templar Castle with their uncle whereas Lily and Aunt Bella decided to look around the church on the shore. Lily was going to take her watercolours and sketchbook.

It took an hour to reach the car park which overlooked the small, picturesque town on the *Côte Vermeille.* Jean-Paul backed into the only free space. They tried to keep together whilst negotiating the throngs of visitors on the pathway leading down to the seafront.

"Have you brought your sunglasses, Lils?" Tom asked her.

"Yes...they're in my bag. Stop a minute, Tom," she said, tugging his arm and trying to root through the mishmash of useful items stashed there. Lily unearthed her white-framed glasses, dusting off crisp-flakes and sugary grains from long-dispatched fruit pastilles. She positioned her sunglasses on the bridge of her nose. The frames disappeared into her

19

blond curls, leaving the round brown, unblinking eyes of a baby barn owl.

Tom grinned at her. "Come on, we don't want to get lost!"

As they neared the bay, the children were thrilled to see a glittering beach, littered with bright-coloured shapes bobbing out into the deep turquoise sea. Babies in sunhats were playing under bleached brollies, whilst glistening, brown torsos stretched unselfconsciously as far as the eye could see.

They all sat down at a beach-café overlooking the bay. The air was filled with animated chatter; snippets of Spanish, French, English and was that Portuguese or Russian drifting into Megan's awareness? She started the game of *How many nationalities can you hear*? The siblings were soon making enough noise to drown out any incoming signals! After a long, cool drink they arranged to meet up at one o'clock before going off in different directions. Bella reminded the children to either keep covered up or apply suncream regularly; the sun would soon become quite fierce.

Bella and Lily ambled through the quaint, narrow streets of the old quarter, looking in shop windows and occasionally stepping inside for a closer look. Fragrant wafts of air filtered through the doorway of a *Provençal* soap and perfume boutique.

"Can we go inside, Aunt Bella?" Lily asked. "I want to get something for Mummy."

White colour-washed dressers were stacked with hand-made soaps, a variety of shapes in delicate shades. Some were wrapped beautifully in pleated waxed papers which came together beneath a silver-labelled seal.

Lily's nose twitched. She sniffed the bars within reach: pale green verbena, fresh and lemony, delicate coral shells that smelt of spring cherry-blossom, rose-tinged ovals that made her mouth water. Were they perhaps lumps of powdery Turkish Delight? She inhaled the sweet fragrance of her granny's scent, Blue Iris, and her mother's fine talcum powder, Lily of the Valley.

"Which one are you going to choose?" Bella asked her.

Lily was adrift in a sea of half-forgotten memories. People and their scents were swimming through her senses.

"Lily!" Bella repeated. "Have you decided which one?"

"Oh Aunt Bella, I was just thinking...I'll choose Lily of the Valley because I know Mummy likes that scent."

The assistant gift-wrapped it and Lily handed over some euros.

They walked towards the seventeenth century *l'Église Notre-Dame-des-Anges,* which stood on the site of a much older church. Its pink-domed bell tower had once been a lighthouse for the old port.

"I love going into churches," Lily told her aunt.

"Why is that, Lily?"

"I just feel so peaceful there. And sometimes I feel the Holy Spirit."

Bella was intrigued. "I like going into churches too. What does the Holy Spirit feel like?"

"Oh, it's like a shiver through your body. It usually starts in my head. A bit like when I listen to Tom playing his violin. He's gifted," she told Bella proudly.

Bella confided that occasionally she caught a glimpse of an angel. Now Lily was intrigued.

"What do they look like and when did you last see one?"

"They're all sorts of sizes, sometimes with wings," she said quietly. "The last one I saw was in the street at the scene of an accident. It was huge, with the most beautiful, feathered wings. It must have been someone's guardian angel."

"I hope I see one someday," Lily sighed as Bella thought how open children are to other possibilities.

Inside, the church was quite dark and cool and a small choir was practising in front of the altar. Bella and Lily wandered quietly around, stopping to look closely at the beautifully carved figures. Then they sat down in a straight-backed pew. Lily's feet were stranded in mid-air so she unhooked an embroidered, blue cushion and slid onto her knees. She prayed especially for her mum and for the rest of her family and friends and for all animals. Bella prayed for her sister and for Jean-Paul and their families, as well as for world peace. As the choral music subsided, the gentle whisper and sigh of the lapping sea could be heard beyond the apse.

Meanwhile, Megan and Tom were enjoying history coming to life in the Royal Castle.

"The Knights Templar built the castle in 1207 on this ancient site," Jean-Paul was telling his nephew and niece. "It was integrated into the Royal Castle in the mid-fourteenth century."

"It's such an amazing place," Megan said admiringly, "jutting into the sea."

"Do you know anything more about The Knights Templar, Uncle Jean-Paul?" Tom asked.

"Well, I reckon that if I'd lived at that time I would have joined their Order."

"Why do you say that?"

"Because they were good, brave men; they donated everything they had to this charity and then they took a sacred oath to honour Christ and protect all pilgrims. They were free to travel and, at first, had the protection of the Pope and the King."

"Where did pilgrims travel to?" Tom asked.

"To Jerusalem and other sacred sites in Europe."

"*I* would have joined their Order," Tom told him.

"Me too," added Megan as Jean-Paul and Tom laughed.

Megan ran her fingers through her fringe and flicked her head sideways. What was so funny? Her uncle patted her shoulder and then led the way through such diverse parts as the underground passages and the Queen's bedchamber.

Jean-Paul told them about the French military engineer, *Vauban*. "He was responsible for fortifying many of France's great towns and cities when the country was at war with her neighbours. Vauban assisted King Louis XIV in the seventeenth century and this is one of the towns where you can see his work."

It was whilst they were up on the ramparts that Tom began to feel giddy. Swirls of colour blurred his vision and a loud buzzing sound filled his head, causing him to lose his footing. There was a sudden clash of metal, like swords in battle, and the cries and groans from men lying wounded and worse. Megan looked around in horror for she could see men in white mantles with a red cross emblazoned before them being slaughtered. Megan's hands flew to her throat and chest as she shuddered and fell to her knees. They were caught up in some other time, some other experience where torture and death were inescapable.

Jean-Paul looked over at his nephew and niece to see that both Tom and Megan were deathly white and Megan was on her knees. They looked as if they had seen a ghost.

"What is it?" he asked, running towards them, "Are you afraid of heights?"

They looked at each other, not understanding what had happened.

"No, we're all right...maybe a b...bit too much sun up here," Tom stammered. "Could we go for something to eat now?"

"Of course. I think sitting in the shade is a good idea too."

They ordered *poulet rôti et frites,* followed by *boules de glâce à la vanille et au chocolat,* and *des citrons pressés* to drink. The children were getting the hang of the french menus. It was an incentive to study food vocabulary back at the house. Bella and Jean-Paul spoke to the children in French as much as possible.

They chatted about their morning, though Megan and Tom said nothing of the strange occurrence. After lunch they went on a little tour of the town, first following the *Chemin du Fauvisme,* leading past some of the views painted by *Henri Matisse* and *André Dérain.* It was fun to compare the styles of the paintings with the actual landscape.

"The colours aren't really like that, are they, Aunt Bella?" Lily noticed.

"No, they're vibrant and vivid. It was a completely new way of representing nature."

This spurred Lily to ask if she could sit and do some sketching herself so they returned to the car to change into their beachwear and collect Lily's art things. They ran down towards the seafront, stepping gingerly across the hot sand like scurrying crabs. They landed in fits of giggles on some very comfortable, blue-and-white-striped sun-beds.

A while later, Tom, Megan and Jean-Paul decided to go for a swim whilst Bella sunbathed and Lily drew. Lily shooed Megan away when they got back; she was dripping onto her sketch.

After stretching out in the sunshine to dry off for a while, Bella looked at her watch and said it was almost time for home. No-one was keen to move.

That evening, Tom and Megan went up to his room to download the photographs whilst Lily decided on a leisurely bath where she would read her book on folklore.

"Tom, what do you think happened at the castle today?" Megan asked, drawing a chair up to his desk.

"Something weird. You heard it as well, didn't you?"

"I *saw* it, Tom; a bloody battle, all the horror of soldiers killing innocent men! It was unbearable. What's happening to us?"

"I don't know but let's look at the photos I took."

Tom took the SD card from his camera and carefully slotted it in. The photographs flashed by and Tom adjusted the sequence to slow. There it was! An image that looked like several shots were overlapping each other.

"What is *that*? Tom exclaimed in disbelief.

"Exactly what I saw, Tom! Turn it off! I don't want to see any more."

"We must be seeing something from the past but that's impossible! I'm going to search for information about the Knights Templar, back to the thirteenth century."

"Let's keep this to ourselves for now; we don't want to cause chaos," Megan advised.

She stood up and stretched, letting out a loud yawn and, with it, some tension. "I suddenly feel really tired. I'm off to bed. Goodnight Tom."

"Goodnight Megs. Don't worry, we'll sort things out."

Tom switched his computer back on and decided to e-mail Andrew, his friend at home. His head was spinning with what had happened and what it could mean.

Hey Andy,

How's things back in sunny, not so sunny, Angleterre?

We've all got off to a brilliant start for the summer hols. There's so much going on here and it's only day three!

There's something I want to tell you though, Andy, and I'm being serious! I need you to think about what I'm going to say. Keep it to yourself and get back to me as soon as you can.

Yesterday I had a distinctly weird experience inside a tiny cell of a church — a hermitage called St Anthony's — that's set into the side of a steep gorge. I don't really know how to explain it but I ended up tripping over a huge crucifix, spread-eagled along it, and then sensing that I wasn't alone! But I was, if you see what I mean!

I was only just getting my head around that when Megan and me have had an even weirder thing happen on the ramparts of a Templar Castle in Collioure! This morning! I'm feeling dizzy just thinking about it. I am not fooling around, Andy, so please read this very *carefully and give me your thoughts on it.*

We were standing on the ramparts — Megs and me. It was hot and the castle does jut into the sea — but neither of us has ever felt dizzy before. That's only the start! We both sensed something very odd. I could hear the sounds of a battle, metal swords crashing on metal, cries and groans, the sort that could only come from men wounded or dying! Megan saw it all! We both went dizzy and white. Uncle J-P saw us and rushed over and took us into the shade to sit down. Then we had something to eat and settled a bit.

But the thing is Andy, we've got evidence. I took some photos and what we saw and heard is on

record! I'll send these to you as well. Actually I'm beginning to feel strange just thinking about it. We haven't said anything to anyone else, especially Lily.
I hope you're able to get back to me soon.

Tom

Bella was so enjoying spending time with the children. She sat down next to her husband on the raspberry cord sofa, tucking her feet up beside her.

"You know, I keep wondering what it would have been like to have had our own children. My mind just keeps going to those thoughts these past few days," Bella told him.

Jean-Paul put his arm around her shoulder and drew her to him. "It's only natural for you to think that, Bella. I look on Tom as the son I never had but we are so lucky to be able to play a part in their lives."

"Yes, I know. The children have settled well, haven't they?"

"Yes, they have. They are really enjoying time with us, which is wonderful. They don't seem to be missing Laura and Steve at all. It's because they're getting older. There is one thing though, Bella. This morning, when we were on the ramparts, Tom and Megan went really pale. I thought it was the height with the open sea view, but they said not. And Megan's so used to heights and holes!"

"You know something, they're all very sensitive children. They were bound to be, being Laura's. But, as I was talking to Lily this morning, I realised that they're very special. Children are being born into the world with far more awareness than ever before. They have refined sensibilities. And I think they are developing spiritual gifts," Bella told Jean-Paul.

"What do you mean by *spiritual gifts*?"

"Well, Lily told me that she senses the Holy Spirit at times, especially in church, and when Tom plays the violin. She senses peace in lots of places too. She's such a beautiful soul...they all are."

"I understand what you're saying. They had that unusual experience in the woods before they came over, didn't they? What happened then, again?"

"They went into the woods in Nether Alderley, looking for healing plants. It was Midsummer's Eve. It's typical of Lily to decide to do something like that. Tom and Megan went with her because they were worried about Laura too, and have noticed how tired she is for a lot of the time. Anyway, they all ended up dozing off under the Old Oak."

"All of them? They didn't eat anything in the woods did they?"

"Apparently not, but it's very strange, don't you think? The outcome was that when they woke up, Lily was holding a posy of herbs — that they *hadn't* picked."

"Now that is very odd! I know this might sound a bit far-fetched, but what if Megan and Tom felt something at the castle from the past?" Jean-Paul wondered out loud.

"Anything is possible. We must make sure that we support them in whatever happens, and try to keep our feet on the ground."

4

No Ordinary Trip!

During the morning, Jean-Paul and Bella talked to the children about going on a trip for a few days the following week. They looked at the map and highlighted several places that they thought would be of particular interest.

"Would you like to travel across the Tarn Gorge on the *Millau* Viaduct?" Jean-Paul asked them.

"That would be really cool," said Megan. "We've been talking about its construction in our Geography and French lessons."

"Is it very high?" asked Lily with a distinct note of trepidation in her voice.

"Quite high — but it's also very beautiful and very safe," said Jean-Paul. "And we will be staying in the car; we're not allowed to get out. Can you tell us any more about it, Megan?"

"Well, it was completed in January 2005. It's two thousand four hundred and sixty metres long and reaches a height of three hundred and forty three metres above the Tarn. And it was designed by the English architect, Sir Norman Foster."

"Bravo!" said Jean-Paul. "You've a good memory for facts. Do you know how they got the construction to meet exactly in the middle?"

There were blank looks all round.

"By G.P.S. It was perfect! Whilst we're up in the *Aveyron* Region, we can call at a tiny, fortified village called *La Couvertoireade.* It was once the property of The Knights Templar and then the Knights of St. John of Jerusalem, *Les Hospitaliers.*"

"I'd be very interested to visit there," Tom said, blushing slightly as he remembered the incident on the ramparts.

"We could stay overnight if it doesn't feel too spooky," said Aunt Bella.

She continued with the itinerary:

"Then there are some caves that we want to show you, called *Les Grottes des Demoiselles*, further east. And on our way back, we can visit a village called *St Guilhem-le-Désert.* You'll love it there, Lily, because there's an abbey church we can go to. Jean-Paul wondered if you two would like to try kayaking on the *River Hérault*, going under Devil's Bridge?"

"*Would we!*" shouted Tom.

"That would be wicked!" agreed Megan.

"We can stay for a couple of nights at a small hotel in the village that overlooks the river...is everything all right, Lily?" Bella asked.

"I was just wondering what you meant by *spooky*?"

"Oh, I'm only joking! You'll see what I mean when we get there and you can decide whether we stay overnight or not. Is that OK?"

Lily nodded her agreement.

"Well, I think that should be a pretty full few days." Jean-Paul clapped his hands. "Good. Then that's settled. We'll set off on Monday morning, not too early. We can pack up on Sunday afternoon and take the kayaks on the roof."

Bella had planned a bike ride that afternoon, just down by the *River Agly* where it met the *Boulzane.* The children loved their bikes. They would take a picnic for an early evening meal.

Later that evening, Tom checked his e-mails again before getting into bed. At last — a message from Andrew!

Hi Tom,

Hope you're all OK. I was a bit unnerved by your e-mail and I've spoken to Gill about it. Don't worry; you know you can trust both of us! We won't be telling a soul, not even your Mum and Dad. So put all that out of your mind, you've got enough to think about. We (Gill and I) went to the library at lunchtime. Gill was tempted to take a day off work so we could really put our heads together — but that's not such a good idea. So we've done what we can so far.

She immediately wanted to find out more about ESP, you know, Extra-Sensory Perception, and I wanted to find out more about the Knights Templar in that area (Collioure) at that time, the twelfth/thirteenth centuries.

Anyway, we're both agreed: keep calm, talk to each other (you and Megan), maybe talk to your aunt and uncle if there's a good opportunity. Things will become clearer as you spend more time there. Gill's reminded me that you had a strange experience in the woods here in June that you all told her about. Can you remember when she came round to look after you that Saturday evening? Well, it seems to us that that could have been the trigger for all this paranormal activity!

*Look, **you're NOT going bonkers!***

The Knights Templar were persecuted because they were becoming too powerful for the rulers of the day. Maybe that wrongdoing is what you're tapping into. We're not sure what all this is about but, hey, we believe that you'll all be OK! You're the good guys! Look after yourselves. Keep in touch and if there's anything you want us to do, let me know.

Andy

The children were ticking off their essentials: Tom wanted to take his laptop and camera, Megan needed her climbing gear just in case and Lily wanted to take her sketchbook, paints and a flower press. Bella gave her a travel sickness pill to be on the safe side.

Jean-Paul and Bella checked that life jackets, wetsuits, kayaks, oars, camping stove and gas, tents and medical kits were safely stowed, as well as some foods and drinks. They checked that five holdalls had gone into the back — with weatherproofs and wellies thrown in for good measure!

They took the D117 towards *Perpignan* and then the A9 up to Beziers, where they stopped for an early lunch. When the family arrived, they parked up near the *Place de la Madeleine* where there was a good restaurant called the *Bistrot des Halles*, sited in the covered market area. One of the delights of this eatery was that there was a delicious dessert buffet to choose from. Jean-Paul and Bella thought that the children would appreciate that.

After lunch they went for a stroll through the park.

"Has this city got any connection with the Knights Templar?" Megan asked her uncle hesitantly.

"It has a very dramatic history and a very similar fate befell the religious group that lived here, as happened to the Templars. Why do you ask, Megan?"

said Jean-Paul, looking concerned as he noticed her ashen face.

"As I looked across at *l'Église de la Madeleine* I felt whoozy and, I hope you don't think this is silly, but I could see people fighting, with swords! Hundreds of people were being massacred, right there in front of the church. I...don't feel very well ..."

"Let's go and sit down over there," Bella suggested, taking Megan by the shoulder and heading towards a bench.

"What's Megan talking about?" Lily asked Tom.

"Look Lily, we were going to tell you about something that happened last week in *Collioure* but we didn't want to upset you."

"Whatever do you mean?"

"When we get to wherever we're staying tonight, we've got something to show everyone. So try not to worry about anything and let's have a nice afternoon," Tom said, trying to restore some kind of normality to the day. "I've got a chocolate bar to share," he said, taking out a very soft Bounty Bar from his backpack.

Tom and Lily sat on one bench and Jean-Paul and Bella sat on either side of Megan on another. Jean-Paul passed her a bottle of Evian and she took a long drink.

"How are you feeling now?"

"I'm fine," she said, a bit more colour seeping into her cheeks. "It's the same kind of thing that happened last week at the Royal Castle. I just seemed to peer into another dimension, another time. It was as real as you are to me now. I could see the most ugly, blood-curdling things. There was so much hate and fear in those people's eyes. Why do people have to do such terrible things to each other?"

That was a question to which neither Bella nor Jean-Paul felt they would ever know the answer.

Bella spoke to Megan, "I think something unusual is happening but try not to be frightened. I actually think that you are gifted, that you have the spiritual gift of Sight. Don't let's try to figure it all out at the moment. Let's talk about it later, when you've had a chance to settle. Are you feeling any better?"

"A bit steadier, thank you Aunt Bella, and thank you for not laughing at me."

"We'd never do that when we can see how you're feeling," Jean-Paul told her.

They both gave her a hug and then stood up, deciding to make their way back to the minibus.

Hopefully the *Millau* Viaduct would be a welcome diversion, Bella thought as the children settled in the back, soft cushions supporting their heads. There was a steady flow of air-conditioning which did its job against the fierce heat outside. Bella slotted one of her soothing relaxation CDs into the stereo. Jean-Paul concentrated on the driving and Bella tried to make sense of Megan's experience.

The fact was that the itinerary included yet another Knights Templar village…Bella was pondering; should they shelve their plans or should she trust that everything was evolving as it was intended? They had organised things to develop the children's experience of France and to give them some exciting challenges. Certainly, there seemed to be strange and exciting things happening. They would continue with their plans…

It was a while later, as Jean-Paul could see the *Millau* Viaduct looming, that he decided to wake everyone. "Come on, sleepyheads, you're going to miss the best bit! You've already missed some magnificent scenery."

The passengers began to rouse themselves from a very refreshing sleep.

"Oh, where are we?" asked Lily.

"We're just about to go onto the viaduct. Wake up, everyone, you'll love this part of the journey."

Bella passed the children cartons of fresh juice, and they peered out through the side-windows and windscreen. It did look pretty amazing, a beautifully elegant bridge looping majestically over the deep Tarn Gorge.

"Wow!" said Tom, taking out his camera.

"Wicked!" said Megan,

"It's lovely!" said Lily, "and I'm not the least bit scared."

"Bravo, everyone!"

When they reached the end of the viaduct, they drove back into *Millau* and parked.

"Shall we try the pastries?" asked Bella.

"That sounds good," Tom agreed.

"And if we come across an Outdoor Activity shop, we'll get you all a good pair of gloves," Jean-Paul said.

"*Millau* is famous for making all kinds of gloves. They export about a quarter of a million pairs a year to all over the world," Bella told them.

"Is there any particular reason for that industry here?" asked Megan sensibly.

"There's a cheese-making industry here, *Roquefort*; it's made from ewe's milk. So, with the abundance of sheep, there was originally the making of lambskin gloves. This has diversified to include any kind of gloves that you can think of," Jean-Paul explained.

With that, the children began calling out,

"Ski-mittens!"

"Cycling gloves!"

"Climbing gloves!"

"Tobogganing gloves!"

"Sailing gloves!"

"Ice-skating gloves!"

And they were all laughing.

After refreshments and a new pair of gloves for everyone, they returned to the minibus to make the journey back along the A75 to *La Couvertoireade.*

It was late afternoon when they arrived at the tiny, fortified village. After parking, they walked up the steep bank and in through the North Gateway, then up a flight of ancient steps. They looked down below. The village was like nothing the children had ever seen before. The houses were made of stone and, unusually, had access to the upstairs rooms by straight flights of stone steps on the outside. These led to a balcony and a door. Bella explained that this was the door to the living quarters and that, in years gone by, sheep had been kept under cover on the ground floor.

Bella and Jean-Paul decided to go down and walk along the main street to *la Crêperie* to have a look at the menu.

"Go and explore for a bit," Bella suggested, "and we'll meet you there later."

Megan, Tom and Lily gazed out from the circular, stone wall. Megan shielded her eyes from the bright sunlight.

"I know what Aunt Bella meant by *spooky,*" she turned to Lily.

"The whole village looks deserted!"

They balanced on the edge of the wall, noticing a small graveyard by the side of a tiny church. They went over to inspect the stones, some of which were circular and inset with a cross.

"The writing's almost worn away," Lily remarked as she knelt down, hoping to be able to read the inscription. She began to trace the etched stone with her finger.

There was a sound like the grinding of millstones as all three lurched with the shuddering earth. A narrow chasm opened up before their widening eyes. A ripple of excitement spread through Tom's stomach as he peered down into it.

"It looks like a staircase! Let's take a gander!"

Megan crouched down to investigate and felt the thrill of a challenge. "Let's go down!" she agreed.

"But where will it lead to?" Lily asked anxiously.

"We don't know, silly, that's what we're going to find out!" Tom snorted.

"But we'll need a torch!" Lily protested.

"I've got one in my backpack," he told her.

"You follow Tom," Megan told Lily encouragingly, "and I'll follow you."

Tom lowered himself down through the hole backwards, feeling the stone steps which were coated in a thick layer of sand. Megan shone the torch, trying not to blind him, but there wasn't much to see.

"I'll wait for you both at the bottom," he called, and began to cough — as he'd taken in some of the dust.

"I just don't like the idea of going down there," Lily told her sister. "What if we get trapped? No-one will know where we are!"

"Look, we can always come back up. You opened the seal somehow and there's no-one else to close it, so let's just have a look. We won't be long, I promise."

Lily got down on her hands and knees close to the edge. She felt the first step with her foot and, taking a deep breath, began the steep descent.

"Are you OK, Lily?" Megan called down into the gaping earth.

"Y...eee...shhh," came the muffled reply.

Megan thought she'd better get a move on. She put the torch into her shoulderbag and, crouching down, felt the width of the steps. Realising just how narrow they were, she focused on her coordination. She could hear sprays of sand leaving her footholds and wondered if they were falling into Lily's eyes, but everything else was silent. As she got further below ground, she became aware of an unusual yellow glow and the air was getting warmer.

The base of the stairway had opened out into a vaulted cavern lit by sconces. Tom looked around him, flexing his arms and legs, and glad to be on terra firma. The reassuring thing was that he could see quite well in the diffused light. He dusted himself down and remembered to wait for Lily who was coming into view.

"It's great, Lily! We've got some light and heat down here."

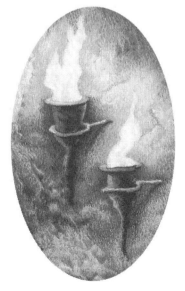

She landed safely and, like Tom, began to rub the knees of her jeans.

"My trainers are full of sand; I'll have to shake them out," she said, sitting on a ledge that might have been built for the purpose.

A few minutes later, Megan appeared.

"Wow! We've got light! Do you think someone's expecting us?" she asked jokingly.

"Don't say things like that!" Lily scolded her. "Let's have a quick look around and go back."

Tom led the way, their shadows were dancing on the symmetrically-arched walls. There were three galleries leading off the main path but only one was lit so it seemed obvious to take that route. They walked quickly and in single file along the narrow passageway that dipped quite steeply.

They must have walked a kilometre before Lily began to complain, "How much FUR...THER? Where are we GO...ING?"

"It must lead somewhere," Tom whispered as if they were on hallowed ground.

"Of course it leads somewhere," Megan responded.

"Just be patient; we're explorers! We may be the first people down here in ages."

"Then who's lit the torches?" Lily asked.

She can be so infuriating at times, Megan thought.

Another few hundred metres on and the gallery widened into a huge, arched doorway. It was built of planks pegged together in square formations and blackened with age. A rounded metal handle, decorated with oak and ivy leaves, stood in the centre.

Tom lifted the weighty knocker and it thudded and reverberated around the chamber. The door opened slowly to reveal a cavernous room filled with life.

"Come in…come in! We knew that you were on your way!" A resoundingly deep voice greeted them.

It was an amazing sight: a long, wooden table stretched out towards a Gothic stone fireplace, logs crackling and flaming in the vast dog-grate. On either side, handsomely-rugged knights were engaged in various activities: cleaning boots and saddles, sharpening swords, polishing helmets and laughing heartily at someone's droll escapade. Megan recognised the regalia of the Templar Knights and just knew that they were in good company. But were they real or imagined? For a few moments she was confused.

"Let me introduce myself; I'm *Gui de Prudence*. Welcome to you thrice," he said, holding out his large, rough hand.

Megan looked up into the smiling face of a very big man. He was huge: tall and broad with a head of long, thick brown hair that curled onto his shoulders. His short beard was flecked with grey and his large shining eyes penetrated hers. Unexpectedly, she felt a wince of sadness deep within her chest. Tears sprung into her hazel eyes as she tried to compose herself, swallowing back the emotion.

"Th…this is my brother, Tom, and my sister, Lily. And I'm Megan. We're pleased to meet you," she said as they all shook hands.

"Bless you for coming!" *Gui* announced. "We sent out a call many centuries ago in earth-time. We have chosen to stay *in limbo,* so to speak, until the places where we met our deaths have been sanctified and our souls released into heaven. There are many souls like us but few like you to see."

"What do you want us to do?" asked Tom.

"That will be made known during your sojourn in our land. We have drawn you here to reassure you that your glimpses of times past are real and there is a sacred purpose to them."

"What's been happening?" Lily asked quietly.

Megan turned to her sister. "We were going to tell you tonight, Lily, but now you can see for yourself — you know that it's the truth."

"I will help in any way I can, *Gui,* but what do you mean by earth-time?" Lily asked.

"Time belongs on the third-dimensional earth where there is Time, Matter and Space, the world in which you are living. We abide here in the Eternal Now, where past, present and future co-exist. This is why we can communicate with each other."

"I don't think I really understand," said Lily sounding rather crestfallen.

"You are experiencing what I am saying *now.* You have moved into the NOW that always IS to join us. It is another dimension and one which you will learn to navigate.

"Didn't Christ say that He would be with us *even unto the end of time?*" Tom asked Gui.

"Yes He did! And this is exactly what He meant! Eventually, the whole earth will shift into this Dimension where time has no meaning. Try not to concern yourselves with what this all means. When it happens, you will understand. Now you must return for your family will miss you. Follow the Lighted Path; your progress is assured."

Gui gave each child a star-shaped badge, displaying a hand-painted symbol etched into the metal. The children had seen a similar image before; it was a serpent twisting around a staff. They each pinned it proudly to their t-shirt.

"I feel like I've known you for ever!" Lily told *Gui*, giving him a hug.

"Thank you for the faith you have in us," said Megan and she and Tom shook his hand once more.

It seemed only moments later they were running down the street to where their Aunt and Uncle were sitting, outside *la Crêperie.*

"I *do* want to stay here for the night," announced Lily.

"That's brilliant!" said Bella.

"Where did you get those badges?" she asked, moving closer to scrutinise Lily's.

"Do you know what it is, Aunt Bella?"

"It's the Rod of *Asclepius*. In the ancient Greek religion, Asclepius was the God of Medicine and Healing."

"We do need to talk to you and Uncle Jean-Paul later and to show you something," Tom told his aunt.

Lily's tummy began to rumble so they went inside to order savoury *crêpes*. The owner had vacant rooms to let which were ideal for an overnight stay. Jean-Paul, Tom and Megan went back to the minibus to collect their holdalls and the laptop.

They unpacked a few things and then crowded into Jean-Paul and Bella's room for a discussion and to show the photographs. The children had a lot to say, taking it in turns to relate their experiences. Their aunt and uncle were very reassuring.

Bella told the children what she thought, "I believe that places hold memories, a psychic impression of what has occurred there. If these things are traumatic and have negative consequences, then they continue to affect people on a subtle energetic level. These energies need to be cleared so that the past no longer influences the present — or the future."

"How can this be done, Aunt Bella?" Megan asked.

"By prayer and maybe the use of crystals charged with healing energies. I believe that you three children, and possibly Jean-Paul and I, will be shown the way forward."

"I think you are very sensible," Lily said with feeling. "You have always looked after us and loved us from when we were babies. I love you both!" She flung herself towards them to give them a kiss.

"Lily, you are definitely growing up since we came over to France," said Tom. "And I'm very proud of you."

Something had changed between the three siblings. There was a realisation, possibly for the first time, that they were a team, that they could support each other and work together and that they had equality, despite differences in age, personality and intellect.

At breakfast, the family sat around an outdoor table. Megan poured hot chocolate for the three of them and they all enjoyed freshly-baked croissants with butter and plum jam. Lily couldn't resist dunking hers into the rich brown nectar whilst their aunt and uncle shared a leisurely pot of *café au lait*. It was Megan who suggested they took one more look around the beautiful yet isolated village.

They crept into the ancient church where a simple cross rested on the plain wooden altar. It was cool, calm and quite spartan. They sat on a worn bench near the front. Megan said a prayer out loud especially for *Gui* and his men, that they would be blessed and journey safely to heaven. She felt a shiver pass through her like a shadow from the past.

5

Camping

They were on the road, heading towards the *Cirque de Navacelles*.

"What is the "*Cirque de Navacelles*"? asked Tom.

"It's an impressive natural feature, formed by a huge, magnificent meander which eroded the rock to form a horseshoe shape. This meander has been abandoned by the River Vis," explained Jean-Paul. "Bella and I wondered if we should leave the caves until tomorrow. We could camp overnight, possibly in the *Gorge de la Vis*. It's a lovely area for walking and sketching, Lily. And late afternoon, when it's not so hot, we could take the kayaks out for an hour. What do you think?"

"It sounds exciting!" said Lily. "And maybe I can collect some wild flowers for pressing."

"Good thinking," said Bella.

"We'd love to do that. It all sounds brilliant," agreed Megan.

They parked at *La Baume-Auriol* at an altitude of just over six hundred metres. From here was a superb view of the *Cirque.*

"Isn't it mag...nificent!" Lily proclaimed.

"Just look at the canyon, winding its way along. I'd better get my camera," said Tom.

"The road's going to be doing some of that a bit further on so hold on to your stomachs," Bella said laughingly.

"Have you done any climbing round here?" Megan asked her uncle.

"Yes, with experienced climbers. As you can see, it's pretty arid in parts, the limestone falling away to form sheer faces, and the bleached rock can be quite dazzling. But we've done some very rewarding climbs."

They went for a short walk and then headed back to the vehicle. As the road dropped down to *Madières*, there was another view of the gorge. The *Gorge de la Vis* was sheltered by the dolomite cliffs of the *Causse de Blandas* on the left and the foothills of the *Séranne* mountain on the other side.

Along this part of the gorge was an ideal spot to camp. It was shaded by a sentinel of evergreen trees, flat and free of stones, and near to the riverbank. Jean-Paul parked and started to unload their equipment. They decided to have lunch before pitching the tents. Luckily, Bella had bought fresh ham, bread and *pains au chocolat* at *la Crêperie* to supplement their stores.

Tom and Megan were following instructions to erect the four-man and two-man tents which were made snug and homely inside with sleeping-bags and liners, cushions, towels and night-wear. Tom went around with the mallet, making sure the pegs were driven in as far as possible.

"Don't trip over them!" he warned Lily.

Both tents had flysheets, to keep out any marauding mosquitoes, and sewn-in ground sheets. The larger one had a small awning for storage. The three girls would share this.

The sisters decided to relax with their books in the shade. Bella advised them to spray on some insect-repellent and keep covered. Jean-Paul wanted to make a fire bowl for later so that they would be cosy when the sun disappeared beyond the ridge. He dug out deep clods of earth that could be replaced and, having tested for wind direction, put a gentle slope on the base to act as a draught-inducer. Tom went to gather some kindling whilst Bella revised the food stocks and planned supper.

When they had rested, Jean-Paul asked Megan and Tom to help him unload the kayaks and all the gear that they needed. After changing into their wetsuits, they took some essentials down to the water's edge then went back to fetch the kayaks and oars. Their uncle also took a first-aid kit, drinking water and whistles.

Meanwhile, Bella changed into her cotton trousers whilst Lily bobbed up and down on the airbeds, playing Pirates. They tied their jumpers around their waist in case it went cool higher up. They both carried a small backpack containing their art equipment. Lily took her flower press and Bella had a camera, map and small first-aid kit. Even a blister or an insect bite could cause havoc in the wilds. They set off with the intention of being back in camp by late afternoon.

The path wound its way through nursery gardens of evergreens, making a pretty sight and a contrast to the higher, more arid outcrops of rock. As they came to a vantage point above the canopy of trees, Lily was ready for a rest and wanted to sketch the treeline.

"I'm going to sit on my jumper," she told her aunt. "It'll be more comfortable while I'm sketching."

The air was breezy but it was very pleasantly warm and they could hear the incessant humming of bees.

"Have you noticed the beehives, Lily?" Bella asked. "This area is known for its honey."

"Yes, I have. I was thinking of drawing one of those next."

It was only when you really looked at an object that all kinds of things were noticed: light and shade, shape and form, texture and tone. Both Bella and Lily became totally absorbed.

It was in this moment of stillness when a stunning creature came into view. She was tiny, perhaps a third of a metre tall. Her delicate features had the grace and beauty of a ballerina. She wore a diaphanous dress of the palest mauve, her golden curls swept back into an elegant chignon.

"Good day to you," her tinkling voice wafted through the breeze. "I hope I'm not disturbing you."

"No, indeed," replied Bella. "I didn't notice you approach."

"That is a bit tricky to explain but I shall try. You were so relaxed in your *travail*, you have fallen through the portal into my world. Lily, you have done this before, in a wood in England. I gave you a healing posy for your mother. Did it help her?"

"Y...yes it did. I should like to thank you...but I don't know your name."

"My name is Aine. I have a responsibility for the countryside, especially the trees, herbs and fungi. Have you noticed the herbs springing up throughout this arid land? There is thyme and lavender, both of which have a wonderful scent, together with oak and fennel, blackberry and parsley — they offer protection. They may be of use to you in the near future. You have my permission to pick some wherever you find them, Lily."

"Thank you so much. But what can we give you in return?"

"You are helping me already, by appreciating the beautiful Earth and enjoying Her bounty. Your love of the countryside is very healing; every living thing, every blade of grass, is enhanced by your loving care."

"Will we see you again?" asked Bella.

"I am always here. You may speak to me whenever you like — and I shall hear you."

A dazzling shimmer of air brushed her from sight.

Tom and Megan were in their kayaks alongside their uncle. He had gone through the safety procedures: they each had a whistle, which was to be blown in three sharp bursts if there was an emergency. The river was calm with a gentle current and it was not very deep at this point.

Paddling through the languid waters, the *swish, swish* of the oars accompanied the changing, rugged scenery. They were keeping an even rhythm and feeling a sense of freedom that comes only when gliding through water. It was a few kilometres downstream when Jean-Paul called to them to look up towards their right. There, the ruins of the *Château de Castelas* were clinging to a cliff.

Tom flicked his damp hair from his forehead and balanced the paddle across his boat. He was wondering how it could have been built in such an inaccessible position. It was easy to dream of knights and escapades in these parts. Megan was imagining what it would have been like to live there as the lady of the castle. In days gone by she would have had maids to cook and keep the fires lit. What draughty places they must have been!

As Megan's attention returned to the river, she noticed a glint of gold by her oar, flashing sunlight just beneath the surface. Without thinking, she leaned over. Suddenly, the kayak was turning a somersault and she was catapulted into the river. In an instant, she was slipping out of her lifejacket.

Megan took a deep breath and dived through the clear water. She saw the shiny object sinking to the riverbed and followed it.

She swished the water and grabbed what looked like an unusual coin, half-silhouetted beneath the silt. Desperate for air, she surfaced, gasped and coughed up water. She waved and shouted to be noticed then realised that both Tom and her uncle's kayaks were pulled in by the riverbank. Jean-Paul was swimming towards her.

"Megan, are you all right? What happened? Was there a current?" he shouted, reaching her and the upturned boat.

"I'm fine, really I am!" she spluttered.

"Let me get you to the side. Just float, Megan." He took hold of her upper-body and, in rescue mode, they reached the safety of the low riverbank. When he was certain that she was safe, he went back for the kayak.

"Megan, what happened? What made you lurch over the side and take off your lifejacket?" Tom asked incredulously.

She opened her left hand and sitting in her palm was a beautiful, old pendant. The strange thing was it had markings in the shape of a letter M and sort of looked like an angel's wings.

Megan dried herself with Tom's towel and got back into her own kayak; determined to carry on with the trip.

They arrived back at camp in plenty of time to sort out their gear before washing and changing into dry clothes. Bella and Lily returned just as Jean-Paul was lighting the campfire. They had called at a farm to buy honey. Tom was carefully criss-crossing dried twigs as smoke and then flames began to lick the tinder. His uncle chopped several sturdier branches, using an axe that he carried in his tool-kit, passing them to Tom to build up the blaze. As the sun disappeared over the crest, the family exchanged accounts of their afternoon's adventures and enjoyed a campfire supper under the stars.

Maybe it was because of all the fresh air and excitement that everyone slept deeply that night and didn't wake until mid-morning. Megan and Bella set out breakfast on the folding table whilst Tom and Jean-Paul started to pack up the camping gear. Lily was inspecting the wildflower samples she'd pressed the night before whilst twirling a soft lock of hair. It was good to have had time out of the car; everyone was feeling relaxed and Megan had no ill- effects from her enforced swim.

When they arrived in *Ganges* later that day, Bella bought Megan a fine silver chain for her newly-acquired pendant. It was another early birthday present along with a distinctive notebook for each of them, in case they wanted to keep a holiday journal. Bella led the way into a well-stocked *Librairie.*

Lily was overwhelmed by the range of choice in the Art section. Eventually she decided on an A4 hard-backed book that was edged in pink and had a honeysuckle design on the cover. She brushed her hand across the surface; it felt like silk. She was thinking how much more interesting it would look inside if she could add sketches and doodles and maybe an occasional pressed flower. Megan chose a compact diary with a purple and gold patterned cover. She could imagine it adorning the walls of an opulent, Indian palace. The weighted cover wrapped around the book and closed with a magnetic clasp. It looked worthy of any amazing entries she would record there. Tom chose a plain black, lined notebook that he could take to his weekly boarding school. No way was he going to draw attention to something that could contain the secrets of the universe!

6

The Message

Megan was reading a pamphlet about the caves whilst en route to their next destination.

"Les Grottes des Demoiselles are underground caves found in the heart of the *Thaurac Plâteau,* near to *Saint Bauzille-de-Putois.* They consist of three parts: the *Aven,* which opens onto a series of chambers and galleries and, finally, an immense hall which is 120 metres by 86 metres and 52 metres high. This is *la Salle de la Vièrge,* the Virgin Mary's Room."

"That is huge!" said Tom. "I can't wait to see that!"

"Why is it called the Virgin Mary's room?" asked Lily.

"Wait and see," Megan replied.

"I'd like to see Mother Mary," said Lily excitedly.

"I think that can be arranged, Lily," said Jean-Paul with a twinkle in his eye.

"Is it dark in there?" she asked him.

"It's lit very sympathetically to the surroundings and there are galleries on several levels to view the wonderful formations of rock. We must tread carefully, though, because it gets quite damp."

"You'll be able to imagine what it was like for the people who first discovered them," added Bella. "They must have been very intrepid when you think that such places were feared only a couple of centuries ago."

"Why were people afraid of caves?" Tom asked.

"Well, they were dark, wet and noisy from water courses and rock movements — and the echoes, of course. And sometimes animals disappeared into them so all kinds of myths and stories grew."

Megan continued reading; "The first big exploration was on Wednesday, 7th June, 1780. But tiredness and lack of preparation stopped them from reaching *la Grande Salle*. It was in 1884, and then in 1889, that *Edouard Alfred Martel*, along with a group of men, explored the caves. In 1897 he reached the bottom of the cave for the first time and, two years later, used a *montgolfière* to help measure the height of the enormous room. The caves were opened to the public in 1931."

"How do we get into the caves, Uncle Jean-Paul?" asked Lily.

"Just for you, there's a funicular which takes us through an artificial tunnel, 160 metres long with a 36 degree incline. This takes us to the entrance."

"I think the whole visit takes about an hour so it's not too long," added Bella.

"I can't wait to get there," said Lily.

"At-a-girl!" and Tom gave her a gentle nudge.

They pulled into the car park and stretched their legs in the bright sunshine. Then they looked up at the huge calcite cliffs. There was an information office and a café sheltered beneath a white triangular sail. It all looked very well organised. Jean-Paul went inside to buy tickets; the next visit was starting in ten minutes.

The funicular took quite a steep path through the *Thauric Massif*. The roof had the autumn colourings of manganese and ferrous oxide with calcite crystallisations. The first room they entered was 25 metres high and they could see a stalactite formation that had been named the *Royal Coat*.

"Just look at that!" exclaimed Tom.

"It does look like a coat, doesn't it? Fit for a giant," Megan agreed.

The calcium deposits reached the floor and formed an undulating curtain, glowing white, from the light of the projectors set behind.

Further on, the children could make out all kinds of things from the shapes of the rocks.

"They look like organ pipes!" Tom pointed to the row of increasingly long stalactites.

"I can see palm trees and cauliflowers!" Lily called out, laughing.

As they moved onwards along the narrow, uneven stone galleries, they entered into the vast space of the underground cathedral. The children gasped at the size of the massive calcite formations that rose up from the ground and hung from the roof of the cave. The colourings ranged from creams to yellows and oranges to reddish browns. There were white, pale grey and almost black striations. They made fabulous creations which had lain unseen for, perhaps, thousands of years. As Jean-Paul and Bella led the way around this vast display, one particular structure came into view.

It was the Virgin Mary holding her child. She was unmistakable. The elegantly-sculpted figure nestled in dripping folds of evolving rock. A beam of light polished her alabaster purity. As the siblings reached the virginal ground, they stared upwards into the exultant face of holy motherhood. She loomed perhaps 20 feet above them, untouchable, intransient and full of grace.

Bella and Jean-Paul moved towards the exit, leaving the children to enjoy these awesome surroundings. In the cave there were small pockets of mist that rose and fell with the incoming air currents. Tom noticed one such pocket hovering above this figure, and then, quite quickly, it began to swirl and enclose the entire form. As the children gazed at this phenomenon, their vision began to blur. The molecular structure of the rock, previously thought immutable, began to melt and morph into human form.

Lily rubbed her eyes and gasped, whilst Megan took several steps backwards in the hope of getting some perspective on the unfolding drama. Tom was trying to understand what could be happening as he held on to his craning neck.

The most beautiful lady now hovered above them; her kind eyes shining down into theirs and filling them with a peacefulness they had never before experienced. A radiant light glowed all around her, highlighting the natural vibrancy of her skin and hair. Her light spread to the darker corners of the cavern and sparked showers of golden particles. She wore a softly-gathered robe of azure blue which rippled and swayed as if the limitless sky were sighing through a cleft in the rock above her.

She began to speak in a lilting, yet authoritative, voice, "Welcome to this sacred space, unsullied by humanity's sufferings. I have Good Tidings: It has been foretold that my Beloved Son, Christ Jesus, will return to Earth. That time is fast approaching. He is awakening the hearts and minds of mortal men. We have an important task for you to undertake. There are energetic portals to be opened around the globe. For this to occur, there needs to be the cleansing of old wounds and scars. Your family will help you — and a stranger. His initials are contained within my own name. We are guiding and protecting you. Trust in yourselves. God bless you now and always."

With this, the Blessed Mother stepped into the swirling mist and began to fade. Now, only the encrusted, hardened shell of her outer form remained.

"Blimey!" said Tom.

"Wondrous!" gasped Megan.

"It's a miracle!" said Lily.

All three sank back onto the lower rocks in silence. They were trying to assimilate the message and to comprehend how stone could become flesh, and why such a person as the Virgin Mary would choose to speak to them. It was fortunate for them that they continued to feel totally at peace. Something of her presence lingered within them; perhaps it always would.

Lily began to feel the chill of the cave and she hugged her arms around her zippered top. It was Megan who broke the depth of silence.

"What's happened just now is almost beyond belief but *we* know it's the truth. We must always honour that and remember the message. There's work to be done and we have been given the job."

She held out her hands for Tom and Lily to take.

They all stood up; they were joined in the deepest of ways. They turned and marched in single file and with renewed purpose in the direction their aunt and uncle had taken.

As the funicular reached the open air, it came to a stop.

"Well, were you all impressed?" asked Jean-Paul.

"Very," replied Megan with understatement.

"You seem a bit subdued; what is it?" Bella asked them, looking from one to the other.

"We couldn't be better, Aunt Bella," replied Lily.

The children were partly in their own worlds; wondering how this spectacular event could have happened to them and pondering who the stranger could be and what would they be asked to do.

St Guilhem-le-Désert

7

An Enchanted Evening

Bella and Jean-Paul were keeping their voices low.

"Something's happened in those caves, I know it has. Did you see how stunned they all looked when they got off the funicular?"

"It could have been the sunlight, Bella, after the bowels of the earth," Jean-Paul pondered. "They seemed distinctly underwhelmed though; and those caves are fantastic. I think they're trying to keep the lid on something."

"I'll broach the subject later," she whispered.

"We've arrived!" Bella turned around. "Are you awake?"

There were a few yawns and the children found themselves parked once more, this time by a river.

"The hotel is just over there," she said, pointing ahead. "So it's not far to carry our bags. The village goes off up the hill. We'll have a look around later."

"Shall we have a shower when we get to our rooms?" Megan suggested.

"That's a good idea. Camping's great but I do like my creature comforts too," Bella told her, whilst running a hand through her tangled auburn hair.

"We could go up to the Square later for an aperitif before dinner," Jean-Paul said.

"Perhaps we could have a game of *boules* as well," said Tom.

"I don't see why not."

The village to the right consisted of a narrow street winding steeply upwards, bathed in the golden light of the late afternoon sun. It was sheltered in the sheer, barren rocks of the mountains behind. Maybe that was how it got its name, *St Guilhem-le-Désert.*

They went into the small, welcoming hotel that overlooked the river at the back. It had a beamed ceiling and was filled with interesting objects. Tom studied the collection of old glass bottles on the huge, narrow dresser that lined the wall. It was the colour of polished tar and some of the glass used was so thick, it looked opaque. Their colours were from a seascape and Tom began to think of what might once have filled these old containers.

Just opposite was the counter where Jean-Paul was registering. He was handed three sets of keys with directions to their rooms. Lily and Megan were sharing. Their typically French rooms were small but very comfortable with bright, flowery wallpaper. Antique pieces of furniture held bowls of fruit and fresh flowers. Lily could smell lavender in amongst some sweet-scented roses. They had twin beds and Lily chose hers before unpacking. The family had arranged to meet-up in the foyer in an hour's time.

There was a tap on the door; it was Tom. Megan answered as Lily was having a shower.

"How's *your* room, Tom?"

"Great, the bed's very comfy. And there's a nice feel to it."

Megan was quite surprised at this last remark but then there were a lot of strange goings on.

"What do you think, Tom? About this afternoon, I mean."

"I think we all must feel pretty much the same. We're in the middle of something special and we need to keep our wits about us so that we don't miss anything important. But I feel strangely calm about everything. Do you?"

"Yes, I do. And Lily seems to be taking it all in her stride. I wonder when we'll meet the stranger?" she asked.

"Soon, I should think. The weeks are going by fast and the work needs to be done here so who knows?"

He returned to his own room to shower. Lily appeared at the bathroom door, swathed in towels.

"Did I hear someone?"

"It was only Tom, seeing if we're both comfortable. You are aren't you?

"Yes of course. I know everything's very exciting but I think we'll be all right."

"Yes. It seems whatever we're meant to do, we're going to get a lot of help and I like the idea of trusting ourselves too. You have to do that when you're grown up," Megan told her.

She went to shower and Lily rubbed her hair to dry it and got dressed.

They strolled up the well-worn street between the sand-coloured houses. There were steep flights of steps leading up to their deeply polished front doors, reminiscent of those at *La Couvertoireade*. An abundance of assorted pots overflowed with rich cerise geraniums and wrought iron lamps reached out from the upper stone walls.

"How many people live here do you think, Uncle Jean-Paul?" Tom wondered.

"Oh, I'd say only between one and two hundred. It was founded by *Guillaume*, the Count of Toulouse. *Guilhem* is the Occitan spelling. After fighting just causes alongside *Charlemagne*, he decided to take

61

up monastic orders. He founded a monastery here in *Gellone* in 804, originally dedicated to *St. Sauveur*. It didn't take on his name until the twelfth century. He died in 812 and had the reputation of a saint. *Charlemagne* offered *Guillaume* a tiny fragment of the Holy Cross, which was brought here. Thus, the Abbey became a sacred shrine for pilgrims on their way to Santiago de Compostela."

"How interesting," said Megan. "Our friend Gill's been there."

"Why did pilgrims go on these long journeys?" Tom asked.

It was Bella who replied, "I think they were people who wanted to get nearer to God and give reverence to Him. Maybe they needed help in their daily lives so they visited sacred sites, places where a saint had been buried or a relic had been blessed and could be seen. When you think about it, they left everything and often everyone they knew to set out on an arduous journey that could take many months. They believed in something more powerful and just, and perhaps compassionate, than they had experienced themselves. They were often poor folk who would need to trust that they would be given food and lodgings. There would be many unknown challenges so it wasn't for the faint-hearted."

"Can we go into the Abbey?" Lily asked.

"Unfortunately, it no longer exists as such," Bella explained. "The buildings were sold to finance the Revolution but the remains have been included in the eleventh century church. Since the 1970's, a small group of monks of the Carmel Saint-Joseph Order live and pray here and participate in pastoral life. It's quite a complicated history as you can see."

They walked up to the top of the village and followed the road around to the secluded square in the shade of an old plane tree. Its trunk was peeling in places and looked like the camouflage jacket of a paratrooper. A quiet café offered a variety of drinks so they all sat around a welcoming table *en plein air*. A ball thudded by the church door; a group of local children were playing an impromptu game.

"What happened in the caves?" Bella asked them. "Do you feel like telling us about it?"

Lily took the lead. She didn't over-dramatise the event but told them simply what had occurred. Both Megan and Tom added snippets of information that Lily forgot with regards to the message. Because of the casualness of the children's attitude, and what had gone before, Bella and Jean-Paul listened calmly and accepted it as the truth.

"What I'd really like to know," Tom asked them, "is how can a lump of stone suddenly become flesh and blood?"

Bella had a great many questions on her own mind so she took this opportunity to find out more details of what actually happened. "Do you think she *was* flesh and blood or was she perhaps a hologram, a projection of light?"

The three children considered this.

"To me, she looked real, alive, a breathing, vibrant person," Tom stated.

"It was the light around her that was otherworldly. It wasn't like the light we get from the sun; it seemed more concentrated, focused and powerful," Megan tried to explain.

Lily added another interesting aspect to the whole scenario. "The thing is, we all felt...feel...so peaceful — and it came from Mother Mary. She looked down at us and filled us with peace."

Jean-Paul had been considering all this whilst studying the children's faces. "You know, when Christ returned after his death, he visited some of his disciples. He looked just as he had done before. In fact, didn't he invite Thomas to look at and touch his wounds so that he could be certain that it was really him?"

"Yes, I know that Bible story," Tom said. "But what does this actually mean? Do some special people have power over the laws of science? Or are the laws of science just not fully understood by us yet?"

Jean-Paul answered Tom's question as honestly as he could, "I don't know. There will probably always be things that we don't understand but you have such an acutely inquisitive mind, Tom, I reckon that you will be explaining it all to us in a few years' time."

"I'm going to have a kick-around now with the boys over there," Tom decided. Jean-Paul nodded and went to see how the game of *boules* was going. The three girls walked towards the corner of the square. There was an arched, wooden door that stood partly open and inside the porch was a notice saying that anyone could join the monks who would be holding silent prayers. They went in and sat quietly in a pew. A group of monks were standing facing the altar. They began to sing. It was a rich, harmonious chant. After a few minutes, they turned and made their way to a side-door.

A monk who had stood in the centre came down the aisle towards them. As he reached Bella, he held out an ornately carved cedar wood box which had a clear glass lid, a reliquary. Bella looked up at him and he nodded so she looked into the box and then touched it. Inside the reliquary was a tiny piece of the Holy Cross. The monk motioned for the girls to do likewise. He then pressed something into Lily's hand and walked back to the door.

Lily opened her palm to find a pendant, exactly the same as Megan's. She wondered what it could mean; her name didn't begin with an "M". She turned it upside down and wondered if it was "W" for

Worthington. Whatever its significance, she was delighted.

As they sat in silence for a few moments, an unusual sensation was experienced on the top of their heads. It was as if they were being drawn upwards, out of their seats. Bella hoped they were not going to levitate. She had read about such things but was not ready to experience it! Gradually the sensation subsided. They quietly left the church.

On reaching the hotel, they popped back to their rooms to freshen up, ready for dinner. The waiter showed them to a table in the corner of the dining room. Circular tables were set with white linen and candles flickered even though it wasn't yet dusk. They had aperitifs whilst looking at the menu.

Bella studied the children,

"You're all looking lightly tanned already. The fresh air has made me feel very hungry, how about you?"

"Me too," said Tom. "Are we having starters?"

"I think we can manage the three courses, don't you? Let's choose from the fixed-price menu. French mains *are* rather delicate-looking aren't they?" Jean-Paul replied.

They spoke in French for a while, Jean-Paul trying to teach them a few jokes. Then Tom mentioned the incident of Megan falling into the water and coming to the surface with a pendant in her hand. Just the thought of it now gave him a fit of the giggles.

A man, perhaps in his mid-thirties, glanced across at their table. He saw, with acute interest, that the young girl with the short, dark hair was wearing a pendant of great significance. He hastily finished his glass of wine and took a card from his inside pocket. After jotting something down, he went over to their table.

"I'm sorry to intrude but I couldn't help overhearing a little of your conversation and noticed your pendant, young lady. I would very much like to speak to you. My name is Michel Ange. I'm leaving in the morning but, if you should want to talk, please contact me on that number. Again, I'm sorry to interrupt your meal."

"Not at all," replied Jean-Paul, who stood and shook hands with the stranger.

"If we do wish to speak to you, what time are you leaving?"

"At eleven o'clock; I've got an internal flight to catch. Good night."

"Good night," Jean-Paul replied.

The children looked at each other.

"What did he say his name was?" Megan asked.

"Michel Ange," her uncle told her.

"And he has some letters after his name: M.M.A."

"He's the stranger mentioned by Mother Mary!" Tom told them, trying to keep his voice to a whisper.

"It's important that we speak to him," Megan said.

"Then I shall phone him after dinner and make arrangements to meet him in the foyer in the morning."

"We'll have to be patient until then," Bella told them, "though I'd love to know what he wants to tell us."

The Abbey Church

8

The Mission

The whole family met up with Michel Ange the next day. They introduced themselves and then walked down to the car park for a private chat. Michel was wearing a lightweight blue suit, his jacket slung over one arm. He was carrying a case which he put into the boot of his car. He brought a leather briefcase over to his new acquaintances.

"Let me tell you a little more about myself," Michel began. "I have spent many years now, listening to individuals' unusual experiences and collating and recording this information. I have travelled all over the world to do this work. Am I right in thinking that you are all experiencing some unusual phenomena?" he asked.

"Well yes, indeed," said Bella. It hardly seemed an adequate response to what had been happening.

"You mentioned my pendant last night, *Monsieur Ange*," Megan prompted.

"Please, call me *Michel*. Yes, you see, it's very similar to mine," he continued, whilst revealing a pendant which hung beneath the open button of his pale blue shirt. "I was given mine by a very special person. You may meet him one day. If you look carefully, you can see the outline of three letters: two M's and an A? They are the initials of the Secret Order to which at least two of us here belong. They mean Master or Member of the Mystical Arts. One cannot join this Order, one has to be invited, and a pendant is given from the Higher Realms. So, congratulations, Megan, on your initiation into the M.M.A." He held out his hand to shake hers.

"I've got one of those too," Lily told him. "I was given mine last night by a monk in the church here."

"Well, congratulations to you too, Lily," he said, smiling and holding out his hand.

"Well done! But don't be worried, Tom. When the time is right, I'm sure you, too, will receive one. The wonderful thing about this Order is that we can be certain we are known for who we truly are and we progress along the spiritual path at our own pace. It's definitely not a race."

"What do you want to tell us?" Bella asked Michel directly. "First of all, how delighted I am that you are both supporting the children in such a remarkable way and to let you know that you have a vital role in these special times."

"We are doing our best and opening up to many new things through the children," Jean-Paul told him.

"I have a map to show you," he said, reaching into his briefcase.

"There is a hot spot here, around these Cathar Castles. There is also a portal here which will open when negative energies have cleared. These portals are forming an Energy Matrix which, when activated, will bring in much Higher Energies."

"But those castles are right near to where we live," Jean-Paul told him.

"I know."

"How can the energies be cleared?" asked Bella.

"Through prayer and the placing of encoded crystals."

"I have a lovely collection of crystals at home. Will they be of any use?" she asked him.

"Yes, I believe they will. But for the castles, I have some special crystals that have been imbued with very powerful, refined energies. They came into my possession yesterday when I visited the nearby *Grotte de Clamouse*." He handed over three velvet pouches.

Megan, Tom and Lily carefully took hold of one each and peered inside. Megan tipped the precious contents into her palm and stared. Sunlight refracted through faceted crystalline structures, illuminating inner worlds and sending sparks of effervescent colour ricocheting from one to another. It was as if miniature pyrotechnics were exploding into her pupils, relaying messages of awesome power and intelligence. She felt parts of her brain wobble and shift; long-dormant synapses sparked into life ready for an evolutionary leap.

Michel registered her response and deftly intervened. "Let's put those crystals back, Megan. It will take some time to align with their powerful energies — and better one at a time." He turned to Bella. "Please take care of them and use them intuitively. The double-terminated ones are Master Crystals. You can use these to activate your own crystals at home."

"You mentioned *Higher Energies*; what does that mean?" asked Jean-Paul.

"Our galaxy is moving through a more refined area of Space. The Higher Energies found there are more evolved, intelligent and aware. They can help us to progress. They can only do this if we are willing to let go of all old patterns of thinking, feeling and acting which no longer serve us. As we open our hearts and minds to this Higher Order, wonderful changes will occur. Miracles will happen. We will move into the Seventh Golden Age that has long been foretold. The process is in our hands," Michel concluded.

"That's a lot to take in!" commented Jean-Paul.

"Yes it is. Some people are more aware than others. But all will be accomplished and then you will understand fully. Don't worry about anything. In fact, this work can only be done when one is relaxed and focused because it is intuitively led," Michel reassured them.

"When does this work need to be done?" Bella asked.

"Very soon. You will know when the time is right. Listen to your inner voice and be guided by it. At the Autumn Equinox, the energies will be activated. It is an on-going process throughout the globe."

"I should like to speak to you for a few moments, in private," Michel said, turning to Bella and Jean-Paul.

The children immediately understood and said they would return to the hotel to tidy their rooms!

"I have one last thing to say that is not for the children to hear. At such momentous times, the battle between the Light and the Darkness is at its most critical point. The Light will dissolve all dualities, to usher in a new paradigm. You are the Guardians of the Light and you may be tested."

Jean-Paul was a little hesitant. "I don't understand...*dualities* and *paradigm?* I'm sorry, but could you explain further?"

"We live in a world of Good and Evil, Light and Darkness, a world of opposites or dualities. Even the average human mind is split between the egoic mind, the mind of conditioning, and the natural mind, which is clear, intuitive and focused, at one with the whole of existence. The time is coming when there will be a shift from this duality to wholeness, a healing for the whole of mankind. You are helping to usher in this new paradigm."

Jean-Paul nodded. "Do you mean the conditioning we are all influenced by: our culture, education, upbringing?"

"Yes, everything we don't respond to naturally, authentically. Conditioning is like a filter, it has set patterns of expected behaviour, responses, even thinking. Our natural mind is free of these things."

Jean-Paul nodded again. "What if we need to speak to you or need your help?"

"You have my number but I also use the telepathic airways. If it is urgent, I shall know. Send me a contact number for the children's parents; they need to be fully informed. Now I must leave. It has been a privilege meeting you all. *Bonne chance! Adieu.*"

Having met the children, Michel thought back to his own youth. He had been born in Brittany and, as a bright student, had studied Maths, Science and Modern Languages. When he was seventeen, he went camping in the forest of *Broceliande*, a forest rumoured to be enchanted. Michel enjoyed hunting and fishing, studying the flora and fauna and watching the dazzling displays in the night sky. One evening, after supper, he was putting logs on the campfire when a few wisps of pale blue smoke began to circle. A moment or two later, a small, unkempt man carrying a staff walked into the clearing. Michel shivered.

"Good evening, my friend." The old man spoke in an amused tone. "I'm sorry if I startled you. I have been waiting for this opportunity to speak to you since the time of your conception. You haven't any baked beans, have you?" he enquired casually.

"I may have...but who are you?" Michel asked.

"What is a name?" came the enigmatic response.

"All that matters is that we know who we are."

Michel was dumbfounded. "Why do I have this uncanny feeling that I already know you?" he asked, looking deeply into the stranger's eyes.

"I am the Keeper of the *Akashic Records* — the records of each human soul. They contain the lessons learned in each incarnation so that the soul's progress can be monitored. I have taught you many things in the Higher Realms but there are still experiences that you need to live through here in order to help Mankind. Are those beans ready yet?" he asked matter-of-factly and, tucking into the warm, comforting mound, he continued, "You and I are destined to work closely together once more. I bring you this amulet."

The charm flirted into the air and came to rest in Michel's outstretched hand.

"It's got my initials on it!" Michel exclaimed.

"Yours is the triune," the old man told him mysteriously. "You will understand its significance in years to come. You will experience many signs and wonders and you will remain steadfast."

He finished his beans and, after saying goodbye, continued on through the woods.

Michel began to think of a thousand things that he could have asked. Then he realised that all was as it should be. He lay down in the warmth of the fire and fell into a deep sleep.

After this encounter, Michel felt inspired to continue his education. He studied Maths and Philosophy at university. From the age of twenty-one, he lived and studied with secret groups of spiritually advanced people around the world. He went to Brazil, Mexico, Peru, India, Nepal, Australia and Canada. More recently, he had worked with groups of Enlightened Beings in Europe. He was always guided and assisted. The time had now come to fulfil his destiny and, amazingly, the children were a part of this.

Megan, Tom and Lily enjoyed another night at the hotel. Lily had done some detailed sketches of the village in the afternoon. Jean-Paul had taken Megan and Tom on another kayaking trip, this time on the River *Hérault.* They had come down the gorge through very narrow cliffs and then under Devil's Bridge and into a calm pool beyond.

They wrote more postcards to their mother and e-mailed their Dad, including photographs. The more dramatic encounters were omitted from these so as not to unduly concern their recipients. When their parents arrived in the *Pyrénées-Orientales,* it would be a good time to bring them up to speed.

Tom, however, needed to have another word with Andrew.

Hey Andy,

I wanted to let you know more about the ESP happenings we've been experiencing whilst over here, in case you can give me some insight into these. We're just having an amazing 5-day trip. I can hardly believe what's been happening! But believe me, it happened! I know you don't think I'm bonkers so can you just hold onto that for a while longer!
First up — we've met some Templar Knights! Not at a Reconstruction Event — I mean THE Templar Knights — and Gui de Prudence, their spokesperson, talked to us. It was somewhere under their cemetery in La Couvertoireade and it was as if he had been waiting for us! We are somehow going to help them whilst we're over here. I know it doesn't make much sense but the next thing will BLOW YOUR MIND!
Yesterday we visited some amazing caves in the Hérault region, Les Grottes des Demoiselles, and a statue of the Virgin Mary, which was formed from stalagmites, just came alive as we (the girls and me) stood looking at it/her! But listen, Andy, she SPOKE — she was so beautiful and serene. She told us that we have work to do here and that we would meet a stranger with initials contained in her name! And we have! He's a Frenchman called Michel Ange and there's a strange kind of confidence about him as if

he knows EVERYTHING! I can't quite explain it but you'd know if you met him.

Anyway, this morning we all met up with Michel and he's into all this kind of stuff in a big way! I mean, he travels the world, finds out about these strange goings-on, and helps people make sense of it all. He's given us some "encoded crystals". They nearly blew Megan's socks off when she tipped them into her hand. We're only supposed to look at one at a time because they're so powerful and they're going to help us to heal places where horrible things have happened! Are you following me, Andy?

We've been kayaking twice, walking, bike-riding, camping and staying at a very nice hotel, here in St Guilhem-le-Désert, and eating some very scrummy French food.

I think I've got to calm down. Thinking about it ALL is a bit of a challenge! Andy, what do YOU think?

Tom

PS. I'm sorry if this all sounds very self-centred. I hope you and Gill are OK. Can you get back to me soon?

Later that evening, Tom received Andrew's reply.

Hi Tom,

If I didn't know you, I might think you're a teeny weeny bit crazy! Just joking, Tom! The thing is, I've never heard anything like this before, EVER! But that doesn't mean I don't believe you. And the good thing is that it's happening to all three of you and your relatives are aware of this. They are, aren't they? It really is important to talk about things so I'm glad that you've contacted me again. We'll have so much catching up to do when you get home.

Take a deep breath and remember...keep breathing! Gill and I have been doing some research. We were stunned by the Mother Mary incident in the caves. We have found several accounts of young people encountering the Virgin Mary. It seems that she has talked to children before!

There's the famous meeting, when Bernadette Soubirous saw her in a grotto in Lourdes. This was in February, 1858. She saw her eighteen times over the next six months. A holy spring appeared and millions of visitors go there every year with the hope of receiving a blessing. There have been miracle cures.

On May 13th, 1917, the Virgin Mary appeared to three children in Fatima, a village in Portugal. She appeared to them six times, and on the last occasion, October 13th, gave a prophecy containing three parts that had to be kept secret for a number of years. This is known as the Secret of Our Lady of the Rosary.

The most recent encounter began in June, 1981, in a village called Medjugorje in Bosnia-Herzegovina. Six children met a woman holding a child. She spoke to them and has revealed ten secrets over the years. Three of these children have yet to hear the tenth. They are, of course, adults now. It is said that there will come a time when these secrets will be revealed to the world and important things will happen afterwards. It's quite complicated and I won't go into everything we've found out.

All these children told someone in authority in their area, like a priest, and I think the Pope was informed too. I'd love to know exactly what Mother Mary said to you. I've got one piece of advice Tom — write everything down. Write down everything you *can remember and how you felt, what you thought. Then, keep a journal including everything of significance that occurs each day with the dates. I know it takes time but your record will be invaluable in times to come. You could mention this to Lily and Megan too.*

I think you are in the middle of something tremendously important. Michel Ange sounds like a very interesting guy. It seems he is going to help you all through whatever it is that's happening. From my perspective, you're all going through immense growth, and there's got to be a purpose to it all.

Try not to worry about any of this. Enjoy the fun things. I'm certain everything will become clearer and fall into place. Gill sends her love, like me. Take care of yourselves and keep in touch.

Andy

Over the next fortnight, the children relaxed at the house, went for bike rides and picnics, and made daily entries in their personal notebooks that Aunt Bella had given them. Meanwhile, Bella and Jean-Paul made preparations for the children's parents' visit, converting the downstairs study into a double bedroom, preparing meals for the freezer and booking a couple of restaurants.

Bella's crystal collection became a focus: to sense energies with their palms, decide intuitively what purpose each crystal could be used for and to concentrate healing energies within them. Occasionally they opened the velvet pouches, looked at and held one encoded crystal at a time. Each radiated energy of a different frequency that fine-tuned their own energy-field and enhanced their spiritual gifts, bringing clarity to their thoughts, conversations and actions.

9

Capital Cities
Paris – Rome

Laura and Steve arrived at *Charles de Gaulle* Airport at noon. They were looking forward to spending a few nights in a city that they knew well. They had been regular visitors to Paris when Bella and Jean-Paul lived here, before they had the children.

After booking into their hotel, they took a taxi to the *Champs-Elysées* to do a spot of people-watching from one of the cafés. They ordered an aperitif, a *Kir Royale,* even though they didn't usually drink at lunchtime.

Laura and Steve had a new closeness. They had spent a lot of time together in the past few weeks; time uninterrupted by the demands of children and full-time work. Steve had been on a three-day week and he and Laura had gone for long country walks, enjoyed leisurely lunches and found time for gardening and even some meditation.

They wandered down the busy street towards the *Rue de Rivoli* to have a look in the shop windows. Steve wanted to buy Laura something exquisite, perhaps a pair of earrings or a ring. They came to a jeweller's and had a close look at the displays.

"Oh Steve, isn't that lovely!" Laura was pointing to a rather large sky-blue topaz and diamond ring, set in yellow gold.

"Let's go in," he said confidently.

"Oh, no, I was only saying..." Laura half-heartedly protested.

"I want to get you something beautiful because I love you so let's have a look," he said gently, putting his arm around her waist.

The ring was a perfect fit and looked stunning on her elegant hand. He paid for it and had it gift-wrapped before walking out into the fresh air, feeling very content.

Steve was going to give Laura the ring over a romantic meal at *Boffinger's*, which he'd booked before leaving home. But first, she wanted to go into Notre Dame Cathedral. As they were walking in that general direction, Steve's mobile rang. It was a man called Michel Ange. Could he possibly meet them at Notre Dame?

They entered the seventeenth century Gothic Cathedral by the North Door. It was vast, with huge smooth pillars and vibrant stained glass windows. Yet it was still quite dark inside.

"Napoleon Bonaparte was crowned Emperor of the French here in 1804, with the blessing of the Pope," whispered Steve.

"Oh, I didn't know that," responded Laura. "Let's walk further down."

They bowed their heads and said a private prayer. As they looked up, a smartly-dressed man in his thirties approached them.

"Hello, I'm Michel Ange. Thank you for meeting me." He held out his hand, and shook theirs. "I have some important things to discuss with you. Could we go over there, behind the pillar?"

Jean-Paul had phoned Steve one evening to tell him a little of what had been happening and had mentioned Michel Ange and the crystals. Now they were in his company, they were wondering what he had to say.

"I will come straight to the point. I have met your children and know that they are the keystone to important work that needs to be completed in the next few weeks. If you are willing, there are ways in which you can help too. It is spiritual work, guided by the Highest Realms. If you go within, you will confirm this."

"We are prepared to do whatever is necessary to help our children and to fulfil our own destiny," Steve told Michel.

Steve recognised that this was the clarion call he had been waiting for. Laura knew, too, that she had been preparing herself for years, but was she really ready to step into the unknown?

"You may have doubts that you are ready," Michel began. "But there is no room for doubt. It does not belong to the New Order. Have confidence. Be strong and focus on the task in hand. All will come into being."

Laura and Steve looked at each other.

"What do you want us to do?" Laura asked.

"I have some encoded crystals here." He showed them a velvet pouch containing what looked like jewels.

Laura had never seen such clarity in crystals. They had a luminous quality and a vibrancy of energy that sent shivers through her body. She found it difficult to take her eyes off them and listen to what Michel was saying.

"Each has a special purpose related to a specific place here in Paris," he continued. "I need to be in Rome by tomorrow. What I am asking of you is to place these crystals where they need to be; to bring about a complete clearing of old destructive energies."

"Have you a map of these places?" asked Steve.

"A map isn't necessary. You will know what to do. Use your *third eye* — the seat of your intuition," he said, lightly touching the centre of his forehead.

This was definitely new territory for Steve!

"It has been a great pleasure to meet you," Michel told them.

"Likewise, and hopefully we shall meet again," Laura added.

"I am certain of it," returned Michel. He turned and walked off through the hushed cathedral.

Steve suggested that they go back to the hotel for a rest and to freshen up before dinner. He had important plans too.

Never before had sight-seeing been quite like this, Steve thought as he and Laura decided to tune into their encoded crystals and the relevant venue. She was wearing her stunning ring that Steve had given her the night before. She didn't realise yet that the blue topaz was the perfect stone to enhance her intuition and channel profound healing energies. They were sitting on the bed in their hotel room after breakfast and hoping to be inspired.

"Let's begin in *this* locality," Laura suggested.

"Well that makes sense," Steve agreed. "But I don't know how intuitive that decision is."

"A combination of both isn't going to go amiss!" she told him.

"OK, I think we should start at the *Arc de Triomphe,* then go to *Notre Dame* and on to the *Tour d'Eiffel,*" Steve suggested. "The crystals should be placed high up because they're going to radiate their energies over a larger area."

"That sounds good to me. I'm going to empty the crystals out and feel their vibrations whilst holding the first place in my mind so will you think of the same place as me?"

"Yes I will. Let's tune in."

As the stones emptied onto the satin quilt, Laura and Steve were startled by what happened next. These were not simply polished pieces of inert rock. Their colours dazzled the eyes and threw up strobes of light that criss-crossed through the air like heat-seeking missiles. They contained an intelligence and concentration of light that stunned the couple.

It was immediately apparent that there would be no choosing of crystals; they were putting *themselves* forward for the task in hand! Laura and Steve felt a strong magnetic pull in the palm of their hands as the appropriate crystal launched itself back into the pouch. When they had finished this process, they decided to book a taxi to take them to these various sites.

Steve used his smartphone to brush up on his French history. *The Arc de Triomphe* had been built for Napoleon I in 1806, to honour the 128 victorious battles of his army. It was also a place to honour those killed in the World Wars. At the other end of the *Champs Elysées* was the *Place de la Concorde,* where people were guillotined during the Revolution. They included Louis XVI and Marie Antoinette.

The clock tower of the *Notre Dame* Cathedral was the perfect place to position a crystal. After this placement, they travelled to the 7th *arrondissement* where Laura and Steve found themselves on the top of the *Tour d'Eiffel* just an hour before sunset, when the view was superb.

The following day, with these crystals safely secreted, they returned to the *Place de la Bastille*, the site of the 1789 and 1830 Revolutions. Part of the *Palais de Justice, the Concièrgerie*, was a prison where people were tortured and killed. The *Chapelle Expiatoire,* within the palace, was on the site of a cemetery where three thousand victims of the French Revolution were buried. Laura and Steve placed crystals here and in other places that attracted thousands of tourists each year. They visited the main art galleries and public buildings, all with the intention of clearing old energies to enable higher vibrations to come in, to silently uplift the hearts and minds of their visitors. It was an amazing whirlwind tour of the quintessential Parisian sights, successfully accomplished with the aid of the reliable Paris metro and the friendly and patient taxi-drivers.

It was the evening of the third day when they realised their work was complete. They were pretty tired and decided to pack and have an early night before their morning flight to Biarritz.

Michel was on a plane to Vatican City; he was going through his paperwork. There was a lot to discuss with the Pope. He had, of course, informed the Papacy about the nature of his visit but there were very sensitive matters that he wanted to discuss privately.

It was two o'clock in the afternoon when the doors of the Pope's private reception room were opened and Michel was ushered in.

"Thank you, Your Grace, for receiving me at such short notice."

"Do sit down, Michel, and make yourself comfortable."

"I am aware of taking up your time, Your Grace, but I should like to tell you my news and discuss another more sensitive matter."

This was not Michel's first visit. He had been received at the Vatican several times during the past decade. Michel was privy to rare experiences of great spiritual significance. The current Pope knew that he was a man of integrity and valued their cooperation and friendship.

"Very well, do tell me the reason for your visit and we can have some refreshments afterwards."

"I have recently met three exceptional English children. There is no doubt that they are in the process of immense spiritual growth. They have been honoured with a task that is vital to the progress of mankind and been given information which Your Grace needs to know about," Michel informed him.

He then outlined recent events and waited for the Pope's response.

"I am amazed and comforted by this news. It correlates with secret documents that are in our possession. I should very much like to meet the children."

"I have an idea, Your Grace, that would align your wishes to another matter that I need to share with you," Michel ventured.

He suggested that the Pope might meet the children in the private rooms at the Pope's palace in Avignon. This was not too far for the children to travel when their work in France was complete and it could more easily be kept private. Also, that particular venue was, historically and spiritually, the very place where the Pope could perform a healing service. The children had uncovered a link between the papacy and the persecution of the Cathars and the Knights Templar — and were in direct contact with them!

The Pope looked solemn and saddened. He knew the truth of these words. It was imperative for him to show humility now, to bless the innocent and pray for the souls of the unjust. He made arrangements with Michel to address these matters at the earliest time as a matter of urgency. They would keep in touch by Skype so that the Pope could monitor the children's work in preparation for their meeting.

10

Steve and Laura

They arrived in Biarritz mid-morning. Steve had booked a room at the very smart *Hotel du Palais,* on the beach. The palace had been built in the mid-eighteen hundreds by Napoleon III for his wife, the Empress Eugénie. In the nineteenth century, doctors recommended the sea around Biarritz for its therapeutic properties. European royalty were frequent visitors for this reason as well as to experience the wonderful climate.

The hotel was very comfortable and in a superb position overlooking the sea. They changed into cool linen and, suitably protected from the hot sun, they went on a restoring stroll along the water's edge. It seemed like a long time since they had felt the hard rills of sand under their bare feet and they began to relax as they stepped in and out of the invigorating surf. It was a great place for watersports, with huge Atlantic rollers and six kilometres of beaches. Maybe they would swim late afternoon.

A while later, they returned to the hotel to freshen up and have a light lunch on the spacious terrace. Afterwards, they sat on recliners and read the local papers.

"Shall I book you in for a *thalasotherapy* session this afternoon?" Steve asked his wife.

Laura wanted to try a seawater and kelp treatment to help soothe her aching muscles. "That would be wonderful," she agreed.

"I'll have a look around the town whilst you're there and then call back for you." Steve rose and went into Reception to organise things.

Laura thought she just might be in heaven. She was in the process of being wrapped in seaweed. She had been showered, had floated in clear, mineral-rich waters, been massaged and pummelled and now, well, cocooned. She was no longer a separate mind and body with moving parts. She was one whole, integrated into nothingness.

Steve wandered around the town. There were some smart shops and he had also noticed several tearooms, but he was really looking for a bookshop. He thought the two combined would make a relaxing and interesting couple of hours. Down one of the side streets he came across a bookshop which looked rather antiquated. He went inside to browse. It was one of those small places, packed from floor to ceiling with books. It smelt a bit musty, *like the pile of old newspapers in the log-store at home*, Steve thought.

"Can I help you?" called a disembodied voice.

"Oh, I'm just looking," replied Steve.

"For anything in particular?" continued the voice.

"Well, as a matter of fact, I'm interested in the Cathars, in the connection between the Papacy and France and in the Sacred," Steve found himself saying.

From behind one set of shelves appeared a small, fine-featured man with a white beard who was looking rather sheepish. "You've come to just the right place. I can find anything you're looking for.

Here's a book!" he said, stating the obvious whilst climbing a step ladder nimbly in a rather long, light-coloured tunic — a silver crescent moon adorning his shoulder.

Steve was on the verge of laughing and was wondering what he was wearing exactly when the small man held out a large, heavy book.

Steve just managed to take hold of it before it toppled to the floor. The cover read, *The Secret History of Mankind* by The Master of the Mystical Arts.

"That sounds like a broad subject," commented Steve.

As the extraordinary man came back down the steps, there was a moment when they met eye to eye.

"Who's the author?" Steve asked nonchalantly.

"I am," the assistant replied.

"And what's *your* name?" Steve persevered.

"It's Merlin, at your service, Mr Worthington."

"How do you know my name?" he asked aghast!

"Oh, I know lots of things *and* I've met your children — on Midsummer's Eve in the woods. Please don't be alarmed. I'm here to help you. Let's sit down and have a nice cup of tea."

Merlin motioned Steve to take a seat next to a small wooden table. Then he disappeared into the back of the shop and reappeared carrying a tea tray set for two. There was a plate of ginger oat biscuits too.

"Do you take sugar?" Merlin asked as he poured steaming tea into two delicate china cups. "Please, help yourself to biscuits."

Steve was in a state of suspended disbelief. He needed a cup of tea — or something stronger!

"I thought Merlin was a magician who belonged in children's books," Steve said hesitantly, looking directly at him.

"That is a *part* of my persona; it's a way of introducing my Self to the young. But there is much more to me, just as there is to you."

Steve was not sure he was any the wiser.

"Soon, you and your family will be involved in a major event of great spiritual significance," Merlin told him. "I, and my apprentice, Michel Ange, will work with you in this; to bring about a successful transmutation of the Dark Forces."

"Dark Forces!" spluttered Steve. "What do you mean exactly?"

"There is nothing to fear."

Focus only on the Light.
Love and Light is all there is; the rest is illusion.

Merlin delivered these words in a deep, sonorous tone which reverberated within Steve's body.

"You will need to contemplate these words and share their meaning with every member of your family. In the places you will visit, the egoic minds of those gone before were not focused on the Light. That is why they perpetrated such evil: mayhem and violence. There may be phantoms of these minds remaining that are still eager to make mischief. They will try to stop the process in which you are participating."

"How can I protect my family?" Steve asked earnestly.

"This is for you." Merlin seemed to reach into the air and pluck something out of it. He handed it to Steve. "It's an amulet," Merlin explained, "with magical properties. Wear it during your mission in the *Languedoc*. All your family will have one by the time they are needed."

"What else can we do to protect ourselves from these Dark Forces?" Steve leant forward whilst clutching the amulet, eager to learn more from this wise, old man.

"You will be carrying very powerful crystals. In each pouch there is a double-terminated crystal; these are Master Crystals. There is one each for the adults to carry. Do not place these; they are to be kept to charge other crystals and to protect you. The children received a crystal in St. Anthony's Hermitage; they should also carry theirs during this work. All will be well," Merlin concluded.

They finished their tea in silence but apprehension hung in the air. Steve had one final question.

"Why us, Merlin? Why were we chosen for this task?"

"Because we know that you can do this work. The harmony and love within your family will make you stronger," he said, smiling kindly at Steve. With that, Merlin took hold of the tea tray and went into the back of the shop. There was a profound silence and stillness, and Steve knew that he was gone.

Steve went out into the street, clutching the rather large tome. He could not wait to get back to the hotel with Laura to have a closer look.

11

A Family Reunion

Laura and Steve were getting more excited as the hours went by. They were so looking forward to seeing their children and, of course, Bella and Jean-Paul. They had enjoyed an overnight stay in Lourdes where they had visited the world-famous Grotto. Laura had been keen to include Lourdes in their itinerary, which had proved to be an inspired decision. That morning they had caught a train from *Tarbes,* the nearest station, and had the privacy in their carriage to talk openly.

"You know, I think we should just take it a day at a time with the children," Laura suggested. "It's Megan's birthday tomorrow and I'd like her to choose what she wants to do."

"I'd like that too," agreed Steve. "How are you feeling? You are looking so much better after your massages and our time in Lourdes."

"I hope it lasts! I've never felt so at ease with myself. I feel really content and optimistic. Maybe it's got something to do with me fainting at the grotto in Lourdes yesterday and receiving this pendant from the nun."

She held it between her thumb and fingers for a moment and then let it go so that it hung by a fine chain next to her heart.

Steve could see that she looked radiant and dared to hope that their troubles over the past decade were coming to a close.

"We'll see," he said simply and moved closer.

Steve carefully opened the faded, black-leather cover with the silver lettering etched into its skin. For a split-second he saw glowing red flames licking its surface and the words, *Holy Grail*, rose up into the ether. He blinked and refocused, then scanned down the list of its contents. There were chapters on the Stars of Origin, the Dimensions of Reality, The Twelve Rays, The Light Body, The Spiritual Encodings of DNA, Soul Mates and Twin Flames, and Sacred Geometry, amongst others. It was fascinating reading and resonated within Laura and Steve as being a very precious book. It would take many months to read carefully and digest its wisdom. They were learning to question everything, all forms of second-hand knowledge. It was important to know for themselves and to evaluate their own experiences.

They arrived in *Perpignan* early afternoon and boarded another train for the short journey to Bella and Jean-Paul's. Steve had insisted that they would make their own way as his sister-in-law and her husband had done more than enough already, looking after the children these past few weeks.

The children were thrilled to see their parents looking so well and relaxed. They hugged each other and kissed in a whirl of excited chatter. Laura thought that her children had grown and changed in the past month. It was no doubt, in part, due to Jean-Paul's delicious cooking. They all looked tanned and well, more grown-up. Bella was so happy to see her sister and brother-in-law. There was so much to catch up on.

Jean-Paul and Steve took the cases through to the bedroom whilst Bella made hot and cold drinks, served with slices of her lemon drizzle cake.

"We've had such an amazing month here with Aunt Bella and Uncle Jean-Paul," Megan began telling her parents excitedly.

"We know some of your adventures from your letters and e-mails," Steve laughed as he thought of the bizarre things he had read! "All of us have had some incredible new experiences that simply defy logic. Let's take it a step at a time and share things over the next few days."

Megan understood what he was saying. It would be too much to go over everything at once and, before they knew it, the whole day would have disappeared.

"Have you any idea what you'd like to do for your birthday tomorrow, Megan?" Laura asked.

"Yes, as a matter of fact, I have. We thought you'd like to go to *Collioure* with us. I know that you'll both love it."

"And I've booked lunch at a restaurant overlooking the sea," Jean-Paul added.

"That sounds marvellous." Laura gave Megan a squeeze. "I really wanted to go there."

"We can have a game of football on the beach, Tom, and build sandcastles, Lily," Steve suggested.

"There's a pretty big castle to replicate," Jean-Paul told Steve good-naturedly.

Lily and Jean-Paul showed Laura around the garden, which was in full-bloom, and took her to see the vegetable and fruit beds. Jean-Paul asked Lily to choose that evening's vegetables before checking on the slow-roasted lamb. He handed her a wooden trug which she began to fill with small, new potatoes clinging to their delicate roots, baby carrots topped with feathery green heads, tightly-bunched broccoli spears and sweet young peas in their protective pods. From the trellises, she patiently picked redcurrants and raspberries and juicy ripe strawberries from their snug beds. *These will be delicious with vanilla ice cream*, she thought. On her way past the herb garden she collected a handful of fragrant mint leaves and several sprigs of aromatic rosemary. All the while, Lily was telling her mum about recent events — seeing Aine, the Environmental Goddess, on her visit to the *Cirque de Navacelles,* camping, sketching and going underground! She told her that, in the next few days, she would collect wild herbs: lavender, fennel and sage to mix with blackcurrant and oak. These would make a compact bunch to use as a protective *smudge* when they went to visit the local castles.

Laura nodded with interest at what her daughter was saying. She felt pride well up within her as she realised just how grown up Lily had become. Her enthusiasm was contagious and Laura suggested that she would look for branches of wild rhododendron, juniper and artemisia to burn as incense. This mix had been used by Buddhists to burn at sacred ceremonies in the Tibetan Holy City of Lhasa. Artemisia was Laura's favourite perfume. It suited her personality — sophisticated and warm yet also deeply layered.

The children played in the plunge-pool whilst Bella and Laura chatted. Steve had volunteered as sous-chef for Jean-Paul for the evening meal and was busy preparing the vegetables. Bella was telling Laura more about their camping trip and how much she and Jean-Paul had enjoyed having the children to stay.

"How was your trip to Lourdes?" Bella asked her sister.

"It was special…unexpected. You know, since Lily's birth, I've struggled with my energy levels and grieved for the person I once was. Can you understand that, Bella?"

"I've never considered it in that depth but, yes, I can see what you mean. So what actually happened, after Lily was born, I mean?" Bella took hold of her sister's hand as she leant closer, empathy glistening in her eyes.

"I've never really come near to understanding what happened to me until recently. I'll try to explain…" Laura glanced through the patio doors and noticed her children playing outside. "I don't really want them worrying about me, Bella…perhaps when you come over to see us I will be able to tell you then. The thing is, the boundaries of who I thought I was suddenly fell away and I was terrified. For a while, there were no reference points…I was lost." Bella held her sister close as tears washed down her cheeks. She was beginning to realise just how deeply Laura had suffered.

Laura dabbed a tissue under her eyes. "Then, yesterday, in the grotto at Lourdes, we were in a line of visitors. I was looking up at the Madonna and, the next minute, Steve was carrying me to a seat. When I came to, I felt so peaceful…that anxiety…that sense of being damaged…had completely disappeared. I just felt…feel…well, content…and very grateful. I'm beginning to understand who I am — and it's such a blessing!"

Bella was trying to follow what Laura was saying. It wasn't the easiest thing but she had an inkling of what she was trying to convey. What mattered most was that her sister was beginning to feel much better after all this time and had a new understanding of herself. We don't stay the same, Bella realised, we continue to change and grow.

As dusk crept through the sky, the men walked down to their telescope, now stored in the summer-house beyond the lawn. Indoors, the girls chatted about the crystals and their properties. They used the Master Crystals to imbue Bella's collection with clearing and healing energies.

Bella had trained as a *Reiki Master* a few years before. She used the natural life-force energy to help heal local people by placing her hands on them. She also drew the secret Reiki Healing Symbols over the crystals whilst murmuring their sacred names and guiding them deep within. She programmed each crystal mentally to help specific people and situations, knowing that the power of pure intent was infinite. Much of this work was done privately and she rarely spoke about it. But she now knew they were all moving into unknown territory and would need all the help they could get.

Everyone went to bed at the same time. Steve and Laura enjoyed tucking their children up like they used to do when they were little. Their offspring didn't complain! As he bent down to kiss Lily on her cheek, Steve became acutely aware of just how vulnerable his family seemed. They needed to stay strong for what was to come.

The sun rose high in the sky on another hot day. It was Megan's thirteenth birthday. Her Mum and Dad gave her new clothes and a digital camera and her aunt and uncle had helped her choose a waterproof watch. She was thrilled. Lily had made her a card with pressed flowers and a framed watercolour of the view above the River Vis. Tom gave her a helmet-torch for caving and a birthday card that read *Bon Anniversaire.*

After breakfast on the terrace, they packed the minibus with the usual equipment and clothes for a day at the seaside. Megan checked her new watch again and took her camera, though she didn't want to risk getting sand in either. There was a scuffle for the window seats as the children got inside.

It was a relaxing journey to the coast. Steve and Laura enjoyed watching the countryside drift by whilst playing French "I Spy" with their children.
"Je vois avec mon petit oeuil, quelque chose qui commence avec un 'C'," Lily began — and so the journey continued.

Jean-Paul had brought an encoded crystal to place in the Royal Castle sometime that day. They didn't want to cast any shadows over Megan's birthday and the children's first full day with their parents so had decided to say nothing about it. Jean-Paul had been reading his copy of *Connaître les Cathares*, a well-researched and beautifully-illustrated book. Towards the back was a clear map of the Cathar sites in the Languedoc. He thought that this would be a useful guide to the work they would be doing in the days to come.

He steered into the usual car park. Laura admired the terracotta-tiled roofs of varying heights and shades.

"It's so typical of the Mediterranean towns, isn't it? I just love these bird's eye views. Do you want to take a photo, Megan, to see how your new camera feels?"

Megan had been reading the instruction booklet and was keen to give it a try. "When we get onto the seafront, I'll take some of all of us."

Steve took the coolbox and everyone grabbed a backpack before setting off down the steep path that led to the cobbled streets of the old town. They ambled down the shaded side of the road to avoid the scorching heat. Megan saw the ice cream shop on the corner and took a picture of all the different-coloured flavours on display, sheltering under a grey and pink-striped awning. Lily wanted a cornet, then so did everyone else so Megan took several shots of dripping ice creams and ecstatic–looking faces!

As they made their way back along the seafront and past the restaurants, they saw a group of marine cadets on manoeuvres with their inflatable boats in the sheltered bay. The anonymous black wetsuits were following orders when, suddenly, the commander shouted into a tannoy, "Overboard!"

One member from each team rolled out of his comfort zone and into the sea; they looked like bobbing seals. The rest of their squad switched into rescue-mode, then spun their boats around to recover their teammate.

"That was just like you on the river, Megan," Tom commented.

"Only you took your life jacket off!" he added reprovingly.

Megan scowled at him. "What I did was totally instinctive; it wasn't tied properly anyway and I was meant to find that pendant!"

"What's this all about?" Steve asked.

At this, Megan revealed the pendant beneath her new white blouse.

Laura gasped, "It's just like mine!"

"And mine!" said Lily and her father in unison.

"Merlin told me that we'd all have one in time for the work that needs to be done," Steve said.

All talk of Megan's accident was forgotten as Tom asked incredulously, "When did you meet Merlin, Dad?"

As they strolled along, Steve recounted their meeting in the bookshop. He told them about Merlin's awesome intelligence, his confidence in their family's strength and capabilities and the twinkling good humour in his piercing blue eyes. They were all flabbergasted.

It was decided an early lunch would be good before getting sticky on the beach. Laura and Steve were pleased with the choice of restaurant that Jean-Paul had pre-booked. They toasted Megan and sang *Happy Birthday*.

"Do you mind if Bella and I go for a walk before joining you?" Jean-Paul asked Laura and Steve.

"Not at all," they chorused.

"We'll only be there, or a few yards further on, and probably under one of those sun-shades," Laura added, pointing towards the beach.

So they parted and Steve turned to Laura. "I think they just wanted us to have a little time as a family. They're incredibly thoughtful."

"Yes, they've always been so supportive of us."

"I know, I've told them so myself!" Lily told her parents.

A soft smile played on Laura's lips as she was reminded, once again, of how much her children had grown.

Jean-Paul and Bella walked purposefully towards the castle. It might have been tricky, not having revealed Megan's kayaking mishap, but Bella's sister and her husband trusted them completely. They reached the entrance and bought tickets. Bella hoped that there would not be crowds of people up on the ramparts. She felt that she wanted time to pray there and also a moment of contemplation when Jean-Paul placed the encoded crystal.

It was the hottest part of the day and there were just a handful of visitors admiring the views and taking photographs. As Bella and Jean-Paul walked along the edge, these few disappeared. They stood still and, with a warm wind swirling around them, they prayed for the healing of all those who had lost their lives or suffered within the confines of the castle walls and within the town itself. Bella asked for God's loving, healing Light to shine brightly in this area and open people's hearts and minds to the Truth. They asked that the Knights Templar be blessed and released into the Light. When, at last, they opened their eyes, they felt a great peace and held each other close.

Tom ran on ahead; he wanted to find the ideal place for Lily's sandcastle. After all, if he was going to help, it had to be something with a bit of structural clout. At the age of almost twelve he was not going down to the beach with a bucket and spade to make a row of skittles!

Megan was taking photographs of the family and the various rock formations that sheltered the bay. She was using the zoom lens to capture the colourful restaurants and hotels behind them. Laura was enjoying the warmth of the sun and reading a John Mortimer novel she'd brought with her, *A Summer's Lease*, which made her chuckle to herself from time to time.

Steve was helping Lily and Tom dig out and build up a rather grand model of the Royal Castle. It was beginning to look very impressive. The circular base was constructed to replicate sturdy rock formations, a slab of compacted damp sand edged in rolls of upright, cigar-shaped structures. Above this rose four supporting levels, decreasing in width, and displaying crenelated circular towers at each corner. Paper flags flapped in readiness to proclaim occupancy.

Tom was boring deep into the sands to make a moat. An idea was taking shape in his mind, something to do with the action of building a three-dimensional structure from grains of sand and its fleeting existence. One moment it's there, the next it's not. And there was one important addition — without water there would be no shape, solidity. Wasn't this a bit like Mother Mary's appearance? Only the missing ingredient between stone and flesh was the breath of life. As he dug with a wooden-handled spade, a glint of something caught his eye. The corner of a metal shape shone in the sunlight. He threw the spade to one side and pulled the object out of the damp sand. Brushing it clean, he held up a pendant. It was one that he had seen before.

"Well, would you believe it! It's *my* pendant!" he shouted.

"Let me see, Tom," said Lily, reaching for it.

Laura looked up from her book and went to have a closer look.

Steve was already confirming, "That's it! Well found, Tom. It's unbelievable that it should be just where we're digging."

Tom put it safely in the zipped pocket of his shorts.

Just then, Bella and Jean-Paul returned to share in the good news. Their uncle helped finish the sandcastle and Lily and Bella fetched several buckets of water to fill the moat. It looked quite magnificent!

"Anyone for a swim?" Jean-Paul asked as he stripped to his swimming trunks.

Steve and his offspring were keen and a few minutes later they were all racing along the beach, leaving Laura and Bella to chat and sunbathe.

Bella told her sister about the Royal Castle and Laura said that later that evening, when they could all sit together and spread out the map, it would be a good time to talk about further clearing work to be done in the vicinity of their house — they could also discuss strategies for working together.

The Royal Sandcastle

The children had great fun in the shallow waters at the edge of the bay. They had a game of volleyball and then went for a proper swim. Steve and Megan swam out further and Jean-Paul kept abreast of Lily and Tom. Megan glided effortlessly through the dazzling waters. When she came up for air, the cool breeze swept over her face. She felt light and free as she kept an even stroke and all else drifted from her awareness.

An hour later, they ran back to towel-dry and lie in the sun. It was soon time to get dressed and pack up ready for the drive home. Bella called at the *Charcuterie* for some anchovies for a *salade-niçoise* and Jean-Paul pulled up a couple of times for Bella and Lily to collect herbs. A sleepy Megan said, from the back seat,
"That was the best birthday ever!"

12

Plotting, Plans and Co-ordinates

They were sitting around the large oak table in the kitchen. Jean-Paul had a detailed map of the *Languedoc-Roussillon* region spread out across it. Bella had a notepad and pen. It was good to be flexible and spontaneous but they were all aware that there was limited time to accomplish the job-in-hand.

Steve knew that he had to pass on certain information from Merlin without worrying his children.

"First of all, I want to tell you that Merlin felt it important that we all carry or wear our pendants."

"We haven't got ours yet," Bella reminded him.

"Don't worry; I'm sure they'll show up when you need them." Turning to his children, he continued, "You need to carry the crystals from the Hermitage; have you still got them?"

"Yes, Dad," they all replied, and went to fetch them.

"We need to carry a double-terminated crystal," Steve informed the adults.

"Merlin said that these would protect us and channel powerful energies. We can use them like a wand if the situation requires it."

Bella brought them to the table as the children returned with their stones.

"Daddy, I'm going to make up some herb *smudges* to light in the castles. I've dried lavender and sage from the *Cirque de Navacelles* and some fennel and blackcurrent from around here."

"Well, that's wonderful, Lily! What do smudges do exactly?"

"You have to light them and waft the smoke around; there is a lovely perfume and then they protect you from harmful energies."

Steve gave her a radiant smile. "That sounds perfect!"

"I've collected some branches from several bushes to burn as incense in the places we need to visit," Laura told them. "We'll need to take a gas lighter with us. The incense will help to clear the energies and sanctify the space."

"That's important too," agreed Bella. She showed the adults the double-terminated crystals and asked them to choose one.

"Carry them at all times," Steve reminded them. "But the most important thing of all is to stay focused and know that we are all protected in the Light."

Now they looked more closely at the map. By turns, they closed their eyes and held the palm of their leading hand over it, moving it and noting any changes in temperature or sensation. Bella jotted down the name of any place where there was a strong response. On her list were the city of *Béziers*, the town of *Minerve* and the Abbey of *Fontfroide.* Then there were many castles, including the three outer ones that formed a large triangle: *Carcassonne, Montségur* and *Peyrepertuse.*

Jean-Paul was well-informed on the local history, especially that relating to the Cathars. He briefly outlined the main points of the Cathar Crusades which began in their area of France at a place called *Fontfroide* Abbey. "The Cathars were Christians who believed in the duality of existence: the goodness of God and the evil of the world. There were two levels of Catharism: the many *believers* and the fewer *pure ones* who didn't eat meat and who followed what they believed to be the example of Christ's early followers. They didn't accept the tenets of the Roman Catholic Church. For a long time, the Cathars were accepted and revered by the nobles of the land and by many of the local people."

"What happened to change that?" asked Tom.

"It was the murder of *Pierre de Castelnau* in 1208, a monk who lived in *Fontfroide* Abbey, which led to the Cathar *Crusade*. He was the Legate, or representative, to Pope Innocent III. Suspicion fell on the Count of Toulouse, a supporter of the Cathars. The Pope was outraged and renounced the Cathars as Heretics. He gave orders that nobles from the north of France should march down to the *Languedoc* region and convert the Heretics or kill them if they refused to renounce their faith."

"Where did they go to first?" Megan asked her uncle.

"To *Béziers*," he replied.

Megan's face went pale.

"What is it, Megan?" her mother asked.

"Oh, I had a strange experience when we stopped off in *Béziers* before going up to *Millau*."

"What happened?" her dad asked.

"I just saw horrible things, sword fighting and people being killed; there was an acrid smell of burning. It was in the square that fronts *l'Église de la Madeleine.* I felt so faint. It was just like stepping back in time."

Laura stood and put her arms around Megan. She realised that her daughter was seeing through the illusion of time into the past. "It seems that you have the gift of Sight. Are you feeling any better now?"

Bella also knew this and nodded to Laura before pouring Megan a glass of water.

"Yes, I'm feeling fine now," Megan said. "I'm relieved that it isn't just my imagination, though. I wouldn't wish that on anyone."

"No, of course not, darling," her mother said comfortingly.

"I think we've had enough information for one night," Jean-Paul decided. "Is everyone agreed that we visit *Fontfroide Abbey* tomorrow? We can stay over at a relaxing hotel in the countryside."

"Uncle Jean-Paul, do you think we could stay at *St Guilhem-le-Désert* again, and show Mummy and Daddy?" Lily asked.

"Do you know, Lily, that's a very good idea. But it's a little too far out for where we want to be. Maybe we can all go there before you go home," Jean-Paul reassured her.

"I've got a surprise for you, Megan," Bella said, getting up from the table. "I baked you a birthday cake yesterday morning so I'll serve it up if everyone's ready."

"Oh, Aunt Bella, thank you. I'll help."

Bella had made a Victoria sponge and filled it with fresh cream and strawberries from the garden. She had placed thirteen white candles on the top, which she now lit. Megan blew them out when the family had finished singing *Happy Birthday* once more.

All thoughts of the strange occurrences were gone for a little while. The children decided to get ready for bed so they gave everyone a kiss and went upstairs. Tom was keen to play his violin, Megan wanted to download her photos onto Tom's laptop and Lily had taken scissors and garden twine to make bundles of smudge.

After getting washed and changed, they met up in Tom's room for the last half-hour before bedtime. Megan stretched out on Tom's bed and Lily sat next to her, hugging her knees. They were almost drifting off as Tom played a soothing piece. As the last chords melted away, he confided in his sisters.

"Sometimes, before I drop off to sleep, I hear music that I can only describe as *otherworldly*."

"What's that?" asked Lily, breaking from her reverie.

"It's so beautifully exquisite; it's like nothing I've ever heard before. It contains notes that aren't on our musical scales."

"How could that be?" asked Megan, sitting up now, flipping forward onto her elbows.

"I think there is so much that we don't know, that we're not aware of, but, since we've been over here, doors seem to be opening into other worlds. There may be many things that we're going to experience that don't actually exist in our world," Tom tried to explain.

"Dogs can hear a different range of sounds, can't they, like when people use a dog whistle which *we* can't hear?" Lily asked them.

"You're quite right, Lily," Tom agreed.

"But why are you saying that the things that we're experiencing don't exist in our world if they obviously do — because we're experiencing them?" Megan asked Tom.

"Mmm...that's a logical argument. Maybe these worlds are overlapping. Maybe we are living in special times and heaven is coming down to earth."

"Or, maybe, heaven is descending and earth is ascending and they're meeting somewhere in the middle." Megan was now holding up two bundles of Lily's smudge to illustrate her point.

"That could be it!" Tom agreed.

"I've always wanted to know more about heaven," Lily mused, flopping back onto Tom's bed and gazing up at the ceiling.

"It's just possible that we're about to find out," Megan told her.

"Marvellous!" said Lily, sitting bolt upright.

"Crikey!" said Tom, as this thought sank in.

"Wicked! Or should that be Goodness Gracious?" added Megan.

They were all laughing again at this seemingly ridiculous possibility.

There was a bit of a commotion coming from upstairs, but Laura was glad the children had had such a lovely time on Megan's birthday.

"Thank you for organising everything so well. We've had a great day and so have the children," Laura smiled at her sister and brother-in-law.

"So have we, Laura," Bella said.

"It's a real pleasure to have you all over here," Jean-Paul added. "I did want to tell you that, from Bella's list, it looks like we should visit *Béziers* and *Minerve* on Wednesday. I just hope it doesn't disturb the children too much, especially Megan. But both these places were key towns for Cathar persecution. *Minerve* is to the north-east of *Carcassonne*, which is at the apex of a triangle of castles that also need our help."

"Then we must go and do what needs to be done. Shall we inform Michel Ange in case we need more help?" Steve asked, looking at everyone.

"Definitely," agreed Jean-Paul. "He said that we could call on him if we needed him and he should be back from his travels now. Though, come to think of it, he didn't say where he was based."

Steve volunteered to ring him. He needed to know that there would be plenty of back-up. Surely Michel Ange would have more information.

"Michel, is that you? It's Steve Worthington. Where are you at the moment?"

"I'm back in *St Guilhem*, where I met your children. Is everything going to plan?"

"Yes, I think so. We've got a busy few days ahead of us. I wondered if you'd be able to help if we need you?"

"Of course, don't worry about anything. You've got the whole of the Heavenly Realms on standby", he added confidentially.

"That's good to know, Michel," Steve replied. There was nothing more to be said in the light of *this* information.

"Thank you, Michel. Goodnight," Steve told him politely, whilst trying to keep an even tone.

"What did he say?" asked Laura.

"We've got the whole of the Heavenly Realms on standby," Steve repeated *verbatim*.

They all stared at each other. Suddenly, this task seemed massive and beyond their abilities. They weren't even sure why they were involved in all this, never mind what exactly they were supposed to be doing. Then Bella had an idea,

"We could choose an appropriate crystal for tomorrow, or several, to include Wednesday's visits."

"Good thinking, Bella. You're always so practical," Jean-Paul told her, and feeling rather relieved that someone knew the next step to take.

They had a look at all the encoded crystals in the four velvet pouches. The crystals seemed to be competing for attention. Was the movement and vitality a form of momentum or did they possess some kind of kinetic energy that was triggered when humans observed them? There seemed to be a powerful force-field which drew them in.

They put the chosen crystals into one empty pouch and tied a piece of coloured cord around the drawstring to distinguish this undulating velvet pouch from the others.

Laura would trim the branches that she'd collected and put them in a hessian bag with the lighter. Meanwhile, Bella jotted down the names and coordinates of the castles that had been highlighted on the map.

"We need to decide where to stay and it might be better to go for a couple of nights," Bella suggested when everyone had reassembled. "Looking at the map, I think we should stay near to *Fontfroide* Abbey tomorrow night and near to *Carcassonne* for the second."

"That sounds good, Bella," Laura said. "Do you know any hotels in those areas?"

"Yes, there's a lovely *chambre d'hôte, La Domaine de St-Jean*. It's in a very peaceful setting, just to the north-west of the abbey," Jean-Paul told them.

"And the rooms are spacious and very comfortable. The house is set among vines and pine trees," Bella added.

"How many rooms do we need?"

"Tom could share with us if there was a family room and the girls could share," Laura said.

"Then we could move on to another lovely *chambre d'hôte, La Maison sur la Colline*. The children would love it because it's got a pool and superb views over the *cité*, the fortifications of the old City of *Carcassonne*," Jean-Paul told them.

"That sounds ideal!" said Steve.

Jean-Paul looked up the numbers in his *Green Guide* and was surprised to find that they both had enough rooms. Bella thought that they could pack in the morning as it had been a long day with a lot to think about. It didn't need to be an early start; *Fontfroide* Abbey was just to the south-west of Narbonne.

They all had a deep, restful sleep, the kind that does not always come to grown-ups.

The next morning, everyone helped to tidy the house and made sure they had everything they needed for two nights away. Megan borrowed Jean-Paul's book, *La Route des Abbayes en Languedoc-Roussillon*. It was good for her French and she hoped to find out more information about the abbey before they arrived.

It was the first day that had begun with cloud. Some mornings had started with a light mist but that had soon burned away. Today's haze seemed to have set in. Jean-Paul felt the heat and humidity could be signs of a real change in the weather. It was going to be a sticky kind of day.

"Let's take our waterproofs to be on the safe-side," he told the children.

They packed everything quite neatly, including the coolbox and set off on the next part of their journey.

13

Fontfroide Abbey

They took the scenic route through the countryside, following the D14 past the majestic castles of *Peyrepertuse, Padern and Aguilar.* This road led into the D611 and the D613, which went straight to *Fontfroide* Abbey in the *Aude.*

Megan was telling Tom and Lily about the history of the Abbey.

"It was founded as a Benedictine Abbey in 1093, later it was affiliated to the Cistercians in 1145."

"What does that mean, *affilly...ated*?" Lily asked Megan.

"Joined, I think."

"Where did the monks come from?" Tom asked.

"Well, you know St. Anthony was a hermit?" Megan began. "There must have been a few of them in the hills around here and they came to live together because the Viscount of Narbonne gave them some land."

"I wonder who built the abbey?" Tom asked.

Steve told them that stonemasons moved from place to place, building huge structures like abbeys and cathedrals throughout Europe. It was very specialised work and took years to finish.

Megan was naming the different rooms in the abbey from photographs in the book when Jean-Paul told them to look to their right.

A massive edifice made from soft pink, yellow and ochre shades of sandstone rose from the earth. It was surrounded by tall, elegant cypress trees and nestled in a narrow wooded valley.

"We could be in Tuscany," Laura said admiringly. "What a beautiful setting!"

As they got out of the minibus, they were surprised by the heat and humidity.

"The walls of the abbey are very thick so we shall be glad it's cooler inside," Bella commented.

They entered the impressive arched doors and peered into a vast room, dimmed and empty, with a patchwork of stone flooring. Immediately, the air cooled and they became more comfortable and reassured. Beautiful arches, unexpectedly elegant columns with carved floral motifs and small, bright stained-glass windows loomed into view. The peaceful cloisters were a harmonious blend of Roman and Gothic styles. Ribbed vaulting spanned out from above, providing a covered and secluded aisle. Laura thought of the groups of monks walking through in contemplative mood down through the centuries. And the cloisters were one of the original parts.

"Do you think we could say a prayer here and place some crystals?" Laura asked her family.

"Yes, Mummy," Lily spoke up. "Let's do that."

Bella took out the encoded crystals and they formed a small circle.

Laura spoke in a quiet, yet clear voice, "Heavenly Father, Highest Heavenly Realms of Light, draw close to us now. Let Your Love bless everyone who has passed, and will pass, through these cloisters. Bless all those who have done your work here on Earth, and bless and transform those who have caused harm to others or to themselves. Clear all negativity and fill this place, and those who visit, with Your Peace, Love and Light. We thank you for everything.

All Honour and Glory be to Thee, now and always. We ask this in the name of Christ Jesus. Amen." They all murmured, *Amen.*

Lily positioned a gentle rose quartz that radiated loving energy, in a spot that would remain undisturbed for centuries to come. Tom placed a vibrant clear-quartz crystal to cleanse the area. Megan placed a piece of refined amethyst to raise the vibrations. They all remained silent for a moment and then left the crystals to do their work.

In the afternoon, the family walked through the well-tended grounds. The Rose Garden was sited to the right of the cloisters; several thousand bushes were in bloom, displaying a dozen or so different varieties. The air was thick with fragrance and the sound of insects buzzing from flower to flower. Megan and Tom took some photographs while Lily sat on a bench to sketch the flowers.

Lily marvelled that every flower head was different. She leaned forward and felt herself slip into their velvety softness, cushioned, supported and enveloped in the graceful curving and folding of pink petals. She delighted in the starry, gold-dusted stamens at their very heart and peered into timeless droplets of dew that magnified this inner sanctuary. Did Aine say that she could pick a flower? Her heart was bursting with joy as she carefully selected three opening buds.

All three siblings walked further round to the back of the abbey. It was so warm and still. Megan and Tom leaned against a stone wall; they were picking up sensations from centuries gone by when a gust of wind seemed to swirl down from the top of a nearby tree, the leaves rustling and spiralling.

"The Holy Spirit," Tom told Megan quietly, and she nodded.

They caught Lily up and were startled by a sudden, loud braying. A solitary grey donkey stood in a small field just a few metres away. Lily ran up to it and called it over. Both Megan and Tom felt somehow awed that this humble creature should be there to greet them. They stroked his head and he nuzzled Lily in the hope of receiving a sugar lump or piece of carrot.

"The donkey featured quite often in the stories of Jesus, if you think about it," Megan remarked to her siblings.

"Yes, Mary rode a donkey when she was expecting baby Jesus, didn't she?" Lily agreed.

"And Jesus rode a donkey into Jerusalem before he died," Tom said.

"I think that is some kind of message," Megan was thinking aloud, "that Jesus relied on a humble creature, one that He knew would do the job. It probably means that He trusts us to do the job that is required."

"I think you're right, Megan. We don't have to be someone famous or impressive. We can just be ourselves and go quietly about our business. It's nothing to shout about or get upset about. But what we do will count. I'm sure of that," Tom concluded.

"Well said, Tom, though the donkey made sure we noticed *him*!" Lily gave her brother a kiss, right next to his ear.

"Was that really necessary?" he asked, laughing, and almost deafened by the sloppy smacker.

The rest of the family came round by the trees, towards them. They had been discussing the stonework and admiring the terraced gardens.

"What are you three up to?" Laura asked them.

"Nothing! We're just waiting for you," Megan told her mother.

Then they ran off to see where the path led.

"I think tomorrow could be challenging," Laura suddenly turned to Bella.

"Yes it could, but today's going really well and we must take things a day at a time."

"We just need to be prepared," said Steve, "and realise that we're not alone."

"Let's drop our bags off at the *chambre d'hôte* and then walk into the village," suggested Jean-Paul. "We need to have some time to relax. You are on holiday after all! We can talk strategies later."

"A walk will be great," agreed Steve.

The atmosphere became heavier and more uncomfortable. They were walking back to their lodgings after an evening meal in a friendly, nearby café.

"I can hardly breathe," Lily told her mum, stopping to take off her white cardigan.

"You'll be all right, Darling. We're nearly there now."

"I hope there's a fan in the bedrooms if there's no proper air-conditioning," Bella said. "We don't get a lot of evenings like this; it's going to get stormy."

When they arrived back at the *Domaine de St-Jean*, the children wanted to go to their rooms. They had photos to download and Lily wanted to paint some of her sketches whilst the colours were still in her mind, though she could always refer to Megan's close-ups.

"When you were talking about Jesus," Lily reminded Tom and Megan later, "you forgot to say how much He loves animals and *us*."

"Yes, He does," agreed Megan. "He truly cares about each of us because each of us is special."

"So, although we may be ordinary, we're also extraordinary," Tom reasoned. "I think that's called a paradox."

The girls weren't too sure but they took his word for it!

14

Strategies

"Ideas keep popping into my mind," Laura confided as the foursome sat in the small, comfortable and private sitting room where coffee had just been served.

"I think we've all got things to think about, Laura," Steve said amiably. "What kind of ideas?"

"I don't know if it's because I was looking through a chapter on Sacred Geometry before I went to sleep last night, but I keep seeing a square base with four spirals, one at each corner. The spiralling energies are related to each other, both diagonally and in every other direction. Then a spiral appears in the middle of the square and grows outwards and upwards until it consumes the other energies. The colours are spectacular and the sensations are vibrant and overwhelming."

"Perhaps the spirals are linking different dimensions, giving access to the fourth and fifth dimensions from our third-dimensional earth," Bella suggested.

"What are these other dimensions, Bella?" Steve asked.

"The fourth dimension has various levels within it. It's sometimes called the astral plane and the lower part is where many people go to after their physical death. It's also said that we sometimes travel to this plane when we're asleep — in our dreams. Anyway, the fifth dimension is a much higher plane of existence and is inhabited by great Beings of Light — archangels and such-like."

"Goodness! I've never given any of that a thought!" said Steve.

"Yes, I think you're right Bella," Laura continued. "They are linking us with the elementals, with angels and archangels, with colours and sounds and energies — the vibrations of the Highest Realms of existence. Those positions enable the work to be done; they are our coordinates," Laura concluded.

"I'm not sure I understand," ventured Jean-Paul. "Are you saying that we need to stand in that formation? Where will the children be?"

"I need to draw it out," she told them, "and you will be able to help me."

Bella went upstairs to find her clipboard and coloured pencils that she used when sketching; she picked up her pencil-case as well.

Steve was thinking ahead. "*Béziers* will be very busy tomorrow, won't it, Jean-Paul?"

"Yes, unless we go *very* early."

"That's probably what we'll have to do. It's a good thing the children have gone to bed."

"What time have you in mind?" Laura asked Jean-Paul.

"*Béziers* is about thirty kilometres away. If we get up at four, we can be on the road by a quarter-past."

"That's a typical male timescale," Laura laughed. "No make-up, no breakfast!"

"You don't need make-up, Laura, and, if we fill flasks tonight, we can have a hot drink and then breakfast later in *Béziers*."

"I'll settle the bill now," said Steve, getting up from his armchair.

"I'll come with you," Jean-Paul told him.

"No, this is definitely my call," he told his brother-in-law firmly.

He was back a few minutes later. Bella handed Laura the paper and pens.

"There's a ruler in the pencil-case if this is a geometry lesson," she told her sister good-naturedly.

Laura began to draw an accurate representation of what she had described. She knew she had to leave room to label each corner. The energy spirals began on the point of each right angle. Her corner was at the top left. She knew that she would be working with Archangel Metatron and with the element ether.

Once she had begun to write, she found that she couldn't stop! She would have the assistance of the powerful Archangel Metatron and Merlin. The name of the Sun Goddess, Brigit, came to her. She also knew to carry the blue stone, lapis lazuli, to place on her position on the square and to wear her blue topaz ring. There was much more but she suddenly stopped writing and looked up.

The other three were staring at her. She looked at them for a moment.

"I want you to take it in turns to talk to me," she told them. "But I don't want you to think about anything."

Jean-Paul wondered how you could talk without thinking.

"Let's start with you, Jean-Paul," she said in a calm, clear voice. "First of all, sit comfortably with your back supported and your feet flat on the ground."

Jean-Paul wondered what sitting comfortably had to do with talking and not thinking!

"Become aware of your breathing, a natural rhythm: breathing in and breathing out. Allow yourself to feel more and more relaxed as you breathe naturally and rhythmically. You may close your eyes, if you wish, and allow your mind to settle. See before you a perfect square with four perfect corners. Now, see yourself standing on one of those corners. Let me know when you are there."

"Yes," replied Jean-Paul.

"Which corner is it?" Laura asked him.

"It's the bottom left."

"And is anyone with you?" Laura continued.

"Yes, it's Tom."

"Do you have a crystal with you?"

"Yes, it's a tiger's eye stone."

"Do you have help from any other Being?"

"Yes...the Buddha!" Jean-Paul responded in a surprised voice.

Laura was writing all this information down. "Which of the *five elements* is working with you, Jean-Paul?"

"Fire," he replied clearly, "...and Archangel Uriel is helping me."

"Now, very gently and in your own time, bring the whole of your being back, into this room. When you are ready, begin to move your fingers and toes and open your eyes."

Jean-Paul followed Laura's instructions and began to stretch his arms. He looked very relaxed and he could remember everything that had been said. "So Laura, that's talking without thinking," he said. "Well I'm all for it!"

And they broke the stillness with a hearty laugh.

Laura repeated this process with Steve and then Bella.

126

The Sacred Square

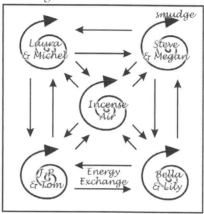

Laura & Michel
Arch Metatron
Merlin
Brigit
Lapis Lazuli
Ether

Steve & Megan
Arch Gabriel
Christ Jesus
Rhiannon
Moonstone
Water

L'Église de la Madeleine

smudge

Laura & Michel

Steve & Megan

Incense
Air

J-P & Tom

Energy
Exchange

Bella & Lily

J-P & Tom
Arch Uriel
The Buddha
Queen Mab
Tiger's Eye
Fire

Bella & Lily
Arch Raphael
Mother Mary
Aine
Emerald
Earth

When she had finished, Steve had an important question for his wife. "What is all this information for, Laura? What does it all mean?"

"First of all, you all need to trust me. I've never done anything quite like this before but I'm simply following my intuition or inner guidance. This geometric pattern is an Energy Key; if we follow the instructions by standing on the assigned points, we will be positioned to experience whatever is meant to happen. I can't be more specific than that because, to be honest, I don't know any more than that. But I do know it's important and I know that I need to trust *myself*."

They all nodded in agreement. They now had all the information to begin their task the following morning. They chose the appropriate crystals and Laura wrote their personal information on a separate sheet of paper in case anyone wanted to refer to it before they went to bed. Each person realised they had access to a wealth of information or what could also be called Light, it was simply a matter of being able to tap into it.

The hot, humid night made everyone restless; they tossed and turned, throwing covers off, pulling them back. Dark figures lurked in the corners of bedrooms and anxieties surfaced from the pit of stomachs. Sweat formed on foreheads, in the nape of the neck and ran down the backs of legs. The children stirred, first one then the other, to drink water and reorient themselves. The adults sighed and peered at the bedside clock. They were all pulled back into fitful sleep.

Bella was flying high above the countryside, skimming the tops of castles and steeples. It was a clear moonlit night and she could see the brightness of the stars and the vastness of space. The long, black cloak that protected her from the cold night air began to flap and fold around her legs, causing her to lose height and speed. As the inevitability of an impact dawned, her body jolted and she woke with a start. She switched on her lamp and opened her bedside table drawer. There was a Bible and on it was resting a single, mysterious pendant. Jean-Paul stirred and asked her what she was doing in the middle of the night. She explained what had happened and needed to know if there was anything in the other drawer. So he, too, put on his light and had a look. Yes, there was a duplicate. Jean-Paul was rather relieved. Finally they both had their own protective pendants.

The alarm rang and Laura switched it off immediately as she was excited about what the day would bring. Usually she detested early mornings but today was different. She went to wake the girls while Steve gave Tom a gentle nudge.

"Come on Tom, it's time to get up. We're making an early start."

Laura and Steve explained to their children that they wanted to get to *Béziers* really early so they all quietly got washed and dressed. They gathered their backpacks and crept down the stairs.

Out in the early morning air there was a low-lying mist. A rumble of thunder could be heard rolling through the hills of the *Corbières.* The children settled into the back of the car with their cushions and fell into a deep sleep whilst the adults watched the hazy countryside pass by, hoping the shrouding mist wasn't some kind of omen of what was to come.

L'Église de la Madeleine

15

The Sacred Square

The roads were quiet, just like the inside of the car. Jean-Paul parked in the *Jean-Jaurés* car park. The children woke up reluctantly and then remembered where they were and what they were there to do. Lily had brought her smudge as well as her crystal and pendant. Everyone had remembered what they needed.

They walked down the *Rue Paul-Riquet* and came to *l'Église de la Madeleine.* The Square was deserted. Laura asked the children to follow the instructions of the adults to begin with, because they had worked a few things out the night before. Steve reminded everyone that they should trust themselves, use their intuition, and remember to focus on the Light.

The wind began to swirl, bringing late summer leaves onto the pavement. Laura and Steve traced out a perfect square with lumps of coloured chalk, aligned to the side of the church. Clear-quartz crystals were placed on the corners. They all formed a circle around the centre of the square and Laura said an opening prayer. Lily lit her smudge and wafted it around, paying particular attention to the corners. Laura lit a few small branches in the centre, using tinder and the lighter. It began to rain, just a few spots at first, so everyone took out their cagoules. The children were glad because there seemed to be a little more air and it hadn't rained for weeks! The bloated drops began to blur the chalk markings but the shape held and the incense continued to smoulder.

Bella asked Lily to stand on a corner with her, and Jean-Paul asked Tom to stand with him. Megan went to her Dad and Laura was just beginning to wonder where her partner was...when Michel Ange walked out of the side door of the church.

"Perfect timing!" he said. "It's just about to rain."

Laura was delighted to see him. She glanced at her watch; it was five minutes past five, a double number associated with the fifth dimension...

They stood on their positions and placed their encoded crystals on the ground. Wisps of smoke from the smudge and the incense began to form spirals, thickening and widening, their form dappled with the most beautiful rainbow colours. In fact, Laura thought that she had never seen such colours before.

Lily asked Bella if she could have a closer look at her aunt's engagement ring. They both gazed down at it. It was a beautiful green emerald, surrounded by eight diamonds. Bella hadn't really looked at it for ages; she took it for granted a little bit after all these years. Yet, it was like looking at it for the first time, as if seeing it with new eyes. *How wonderful would that be*, she thought, *if I could wake up each morning and see the world as if for the first time.* As she contemplated this, she felt a sensation of everything beginning to slip away. Was she about to faint, she wondered? But she had never fainted in her life. No, she would just go with this unfamiliar feeling.

Every atom of her body began to vibrate. It was a sensation that began in her head and gradually spread throughout her entire being, building up momentum to a critical pitch. She found herself in a tunnel of light with the sensation of being able to let go and trust the process.

She did not resist.

Steve was standing with Megan and it began to rain heavily. He told Megan to pull up her hood and then looked upwards into the sky. He'd never actually looked up into raindrops before. They were not simply droplets of colourless water; they were tinged with light. Delicate colours bounced off them, mixing and forming new shades. They sparkled and refracted the light. Steve was mesmerised. He felt a bit shivery and, somehow, a bit freer in his body. He got the distinct impression that he was moving upwards, perhaps through clouds. But how could that be?

He decided not to worry about it.

Jean-Paul was standing with Tom. The thunder was getting louder and rain was splashing up from the ground. Suddenly, there was an ear-cracking sound and an almost blinding flash of lightning right where they were standing. For a horrible moment, Jean-Paul thought they had been struck. He would never forgive himself if anything happened to Tom. He felt somehow stunned; his mind became completely still. He was lying somewhere, feeling very peaceful, and there was the most sublime music.

Tom would definitely love this place, he thought.

"I'm glad that you have seen the beauty in the smallest drops of water, Steve," a gentle voice came through the white mist.

Steve looked around; everything was white, formless, nameless.

"Where am I? Who are you?" he asked.

"I have many names and am known by very few," came the enigmatic response. "You are safe here with me," it continued.

"Why am I here?" Steve asked, trying to keep a rising panic from his voice. Whatever had happened to Megan?

"It is where you truly belong, in the present — in my presence," the voice said soothingly. "Don't be alarmed. All will become clear. Trust. When you have rested I have a few things to show you."

Steve didn't know what to do. This was an unfamiliar situation to be in. He *always* knew what to do. There was always *something* to do. Where was *everybody*? Where was *everything*? What could he do by himself? Then Steve had a thought, *focus only on the Light.*

A warm sensation began to spread from the centre of his chest; it filled him with a feeling of peace. A beautiful, huge figure came into view. There was no doubt about it, it was an angel: feathered wings spread outwards and upwards above a haloed head, golden curls fell to translucent folds that draped the shoulders of this vast Being of Light.

"My name is Gabriel," the melodious tones floated on a current of air. "I have come to help you. How are you feeling?"

"I'm feeling comfortable."

"Then, we shall begin."

A large screen appeared in front of him and an overview of his life began to roll over it. Steve became aware of the intentions, emotions and consequences relating to his choices and actions. He remained somehow detached, yet better informed and more aware of the details of his life. The screen went blank.

"How are you feeling?" The question was repeated.

134

"Content; I've had a good life and done my best," Steve commented without guile.

"There is something more that you need to experience," Archangel Gabriel told him.

Bella found herself in a light, airy room with a shaft of blue-white light coming through a circular window. It reminded her of the cloisters at *Fontfroide* Abbey. She was still thinking of her engagement ring, though; when she looked down, she didn't appear to be wearing it.

"Don't worry," a loving voice came from the direction of the window. "You have *lost* nothing."

As Bella gazed into the light, she saw the distinct shape of a beautiful lady whom she knew to be Mother Mary.

"I just wanted to talk to you," Mother Mary continued. "There is a pain in your heart that you have not been able to let go."

Bella's eyes filled with tears. She began to sob; her chest felt constricted and heavy. She had miscarried a child when a student at the *Sorbonne*; it was Jean-Paul's child. Somehow they had never been able to discuss it. In a very selfish way, it had been a blessing. They had both been able to continue their studies and qualify but it was a child that they now longed for.

"All is well," Mother Mary told her. "You will see and know the truth of these words."

The apparition disappeared and Bella felt at peace, an ease within herself that flowed through her body.

A moment later, an angelic Being appeared beside her. There was great warmth emanating from him. His blue eyes shone with loving awareness.

"Bella, my name is Raphael. How are you feeling?"

"I'm honoured to be in your presence," she began. "I feel that a weight has been lifted from my heart."

"God is very pleased with you. There is something that He wants you to see."

Jean-Paul opened his eyes from a dream-like state. He was exactly where he loved to be — out in the open countryside. He noticed that he was wearing his climbing gear and there was what looked suspiciously like a mountain in the far distance. Phew! It was going to be a long trek, even to get to base camp. But where was the rest of his team? He loved the camaraderie and he appreciated the team spirit. He felt a bit isolated; how come he was on his own?

"Some things can only be done alone," said a voice.

Jean-Paul looked behind him. He was alone.

"You can do it," the same voice said.

Jean-Paul looked around again. He had to face the fact that this voice was possibly coming from inside his own head. "Who are you?" Jean-Paul asked.

"That is a very good question. Don't you mean, *who am I?*"

Jean-Paul repeated this question. "Who am I?" He said this earnestly and with a deep intention of discovering the answer. Suddenly, nothing seemed as important as the answer to this question. In a dazzling moment, Jean-Paul had a deep realisation; he was *everything*, there was *no* separation!

He gazed around in wonder. Everything was alive, vibrant and perfect. It was all a part of him and he was in everything. He began to laugh; he positively roared with laughter until his sides ached! He rolled into the soft grass and inspected *every* blade; they were all *perfect*. He was perfect.

Everything had always been perfect and always would be.

At this moment, another figure appeared before him. The relaxed and well-rounded person was sitting in what Jean-Paul knew to be the *lotus posture.*

"Welcome to the New Earth, Jean-Paul. My name is Maitreya," he beamed jovially. It was Lord Maitreya, the Bringer of Joy. "How are you feeling?"

"I've never felt better, my Lord," Jean-Paul replied, trying to contain his mirth.

"I am delighted with your progress and your new-found awareness; you have come a long way. Now you know what is possible and what has been decreed for the Earth and Mankind. Use your new gift wisely," Lord Maitreya advised. "God has work for you to do when you return home.

But first, there is something that He wants you to see."

Laura was in the *Fifth Dimension.* She was bathed in a glorious, golden orange light which emanated from a Universal Being.

"Welcome. My name is Metatron. You are a High Priestess of the Light, Laura, and ready to receive my Cloak of Light. It will assist you and others in your Ascension."

"I am honoured to accept it, Archangel Metatron."

"I'm very pleased with your mathematical skills," he told her. "Thank you. I wasn't really aware of *studying* Sacred Geometry, I just find it so fascinating."

"That is the best way to learn, focusing on those things that you are passionate about, things that bring you joy and fulfilment. Now that you are here, let me explain something further. You know that you have been responsible for devising an energetic pathway for your entire family to progress spiritually, don't you?"

"Well, n...no...I wasn't aware of that, exactly."

"Let me show you what you have achieved. Please take a seat, Laura, and be prepared for an inter-stellar journey."

The seat reclined and her line of vision was now directed towards the Heavens. As Laura relaxed, she became a part of the creative energy of the Universe. She experienced the awesome power that governed the Heavenly Bodies: creating and collapsing galaxies, transforming tiny particles of matter into the recognisable building blocks of existence. The colours of the cosmos were spectacular and she could hear sublime music. Laura experienced her own energetic birth from the star Sirius. She was intrigued and awed to see one particle of light split into two and go their separate ways: developing and transforming, communing and transmuting, colliding and brightening. She was a radiant point of light, ever expanding, ever morphing.

Laura was aware of other points of light emanating from other stars, their trajectories crossing and interconnecting and regenerating. She saw the planet earth coming towards her and the realisation that this was a new kind of birth — one born into the world of matter.

Laura sensed Merlin's presence and telepathically heard his communication:

"You have been brought back from your place of a thousand worlds away in the cosmos to be present on Earth at this time, to help with the transformation of the Earth itself, away from being a materialistic place with many negative emotions surrounding it and move towards that which is truly spiritual.

By learning the difficult lessons on Earth, life-time after life-time, our human soul begins to comprehend the vast scope of existence in the infinite Universe. The human embryo itself, while preparing for its entry into this Earth, captures with it an entire evolution of life on this planet: as it firstly resembles reptilian, and then through to the Earth-form. The embryo contains all the meaningful experiences gained in this passage. You are now preparing for a rebirth — into the world of spirit.

Remain seated, Laura, there is something I want you to see."

16

A Rendezvous

Megan, Tom and Lily found themselves in the middle of a clearing with Merlin.

"Welcome, children, welcome!" he said with arms outstretched. "My name is Merlin and we have met before though you might not yet remember."

The children did think he looked familiar — and he certainly looked like a wizard!

Megan spoke first, "We're pleased to meet you, Merlin, but we're a bit disorientated. We were just standing in front of a church in *Béziers*."

"What's happened to Mummy and Daddy, and Aunt Bella and Uncle Jean-Paul?" Lily asked him, looking as though she were about to burst into tears.

"Don't worry about a thing," Merlin said, moving towards her to take her hand. "There's someone else, who you *do* know, about to join us. Then we'll both explain."

A young man with dark, curly hair appeared in a vortex of energy. It was Michel Ange!

"Hello there," he said with a welcoming smile.

"Hello Michel," said Tom, stepping towards him.

"How are you all? I'm so glad that you've made it here."

"Would you like something to eat?" Merlin asked them. "I know you didn't have time for much

141

breakfast this morning." He motioned to them to sit at a wooden picnic table set beneath an oak. There was a delicious array of tasty morsels and divine juices. He offered them a colourful dish of forest fruits, knowing how young folk prefer healthy food! Merlin smiled wryly and tucked into slivers of greengage and shallot, dipped in honey. "I haven't eaten in years!" he told them with a chuckle.

"Please don't worry about the rest of your family," Michel explained, sensing their unease. "I've just left your mother and she is having a meeting with some very senior Light Beings. There are more things for you all to experience and then you will be reunited."

Comforted by his explanation, the children started to eat the delicious food provided, suddenly realising that they hadn't eaten since dinner the previous evening which seemed a very long time ago.

"Can you remember that day in the woods near to your home?" Merlin asked. "You came into this world then, but I cast a gentle spell of forgetfulness over you before you left to protect your fragile awareness. You have all grown since then. Do you think you are ready to remember?" he asked them.

"Yes, I think so," Tom agreed, looking at his sisters for confirmation.

Merlin murmured an incantation and sparks of light surrounded the children's heads, forming haloes. They became aware of a magical new world, filled with vibrant beings, colour, light and activity surrounding them.

Pixies were industriously cultivating vegetable plots which were over-flowing with healthy, ripe produce. Fairies were helping the bees to collect nectar for bumper crops of honey. Water nymphs were bathing in the sparkling waters of ponds, filled by recent heavenly showers. There was a gentle hum of harmony and purpose within the Elemental Realms.

"Michel and I would like you to meet the Coordinators of this Realm, if you will come this way."

They followed him to a circular clump of trees. Through the lower branches they peered in to see something amazing…

Titania and Oberon sat at an exquisite circular quartz table, where sunlight refracted a myriad of beautiful colours through its faceted edge. Around it were gathering esteemed members of the Elemental and Higher Realms. Aine, the Celtic Fairy Queen, wore a lavender-scented robe, her golden locks swept upwards into a crystal comb. Coloured sparks of light darted minnow-like, forming a halo around her delicate features. She carried a pomander of woodland leaves: oak, hawthorn, ash, birch and mistletoe and a sweet mix of herbs. She also carried a responsibility for the vital spark of Life.

Rhiannon, the Welsh Moon Goddess, appeared on a white horse. Her opalescent gown shimmered in the sunlight; its bodice gathered at the heart in a huge circular moonstone which reflected back to her the emotional state of mankind. She alighted from her steed and, with a gracious smile, greeted those present.

Next came Brigit, the Sun Goddess, through a portal of flaming light. Her auburn ringlets gleamed. She was dressed in emerald folds of silk with an embroidered mantle of sage velvet. Its symbols radiated the energy of the goddess's special interests: craftwork, creativity, prophecy and healing. Brigit descended to the Elemental Realms and acknowledged the spirit of each being.

Queen Mab, the fairies' midwife and conveyor of mortal souls to the Higher Realms, drove through the ether in her silent carriage, cobalt pennons flying. She had travelled through time and space to this momentous meeting. The majestic carriage slowed and the elegant Queen floated into view. A fan-like collar of purple-pleated gauze framed her pale complexion and her dark eyes shone with a depth of sensitivity and compassion. She was here to help with the rebirth of Mankind.

The Oak King, standing to one side, drew himself up to his full, magnificent stature. He wore a crown of acorns intertwined with leaves and twigs and carried a mace carved from the finest oak, which he struck on the ground three times. A shiver rippled through the forest. He represented all trees and greenery from Yule to Midsummer.

"Queen Titania, King Oberon, fairies, elves, nymphs and sprites and all Beings of Light, I feel impelled to speak. It is the day that I traditionally hand over my care-taking duties to the Holly King. Alas, we are overwhelmed with negativity. Pollution, destruction and carelessness have tipped the balance of our ecology towards disaster. Countless acres of forest are being destroyed. Chemicals and waste are polluting our rivers, lakes and seas. We are being swept from the Earth. Are we no longer valued for who we are?

"We enrich the air for sentient beings to breathe. We provide shelter, warmth and comfort. Our wood makes beautiful furniture, musical instruments, books and artefacts to spread knowledge and uplift the spirit. The Earth is groaning beneath the weight of refuse dumped into her scars. We need to act quickly to save this beautiful Terra."

Titania's crystal voice rang out, delicate yet clear.

144

"Mighty Oak King, we hear your pleas. The purpose of this meeting is to discuss and resolve these concerns. As you know, King Oberon and I have been collating information from all corners of our realm. We have contacted the highest Beings of Light to join us today in coordinating a series of actions, which will help to bring about the next step in our evolution.

A beam of violet light that danced on Titania's crown swiftly moved to Rhiannon's forehead and she began to speak:

"For many moons I have observed and felt the levels of emotion within the human race. There is much anger, frustration and sadness. It rises like black clouds from homes, schools and workplaces. The layer is now so dense that super-charged crystals are needed to discharge the energy and transmute its frequency. Then more refined energies of acceptance, gratitude and love can be beamed through these crystals into the hearts and minds of Mankind. I can prepare the Earth's crystal deposits in readiness for future events."

The violet ray danced and shot towards Queen Mab. It pierced her brow and her dark eyes opened wide.

"Many souls are in limbo, stuck in the Earth's energetic field. They cannot ascend since the earth-cord is weighted with unresolved matters of the heart: judgements, sadness and regrets. Help is needed in counselling and compassion to prepare those ready to depart. I can work with these souls with the help of their guardian angels, guides and the Archangelic Realms."

The sparkling light around Aine changed to violet. She acknowledged inwardly her empowerment and stated clearly,

"I have special responsibilities for the environment and the protection of diverse species.

145

My magical herbs, balms and potions will have their part to play. I shall work with the Elemental Realms to cleanse, nurture and enchant, using the bounty of the woodlands. I shall inspire the hearts of those wishing to work with natural medicines and herbs. They will gain knowledge and confidence in their use and witness wonderful growth and healings."

An amethyst disc swirled through the still air and landed on Brigit's *third eye*. Her mantle fluttered and each symbol vibrated with renewed energy. She rose to speak.

"My concern is for the development of human potential. I shall promote the hidden talents that lie dormant within the depths of human hearts. I shall work tirelessly to inspire individuals to use their creative abilities and express themselves through poetry, arts and crafts. I shall protect the harvests and farm animals to provide nutritious meals.

The glowing amethyst dissolved, and flashes of light surrounded Oberon, crackling like sparklers.

"My Lady Titania, honoured guests and Highest Realms of Light, I am overwhelmed by the vast and powerful assistance that you are offering in such gentle and appropriate ways. May I offer you refreshments before we reconvene."

The fairies and elves, with a little help from the Kingdom of Magic, provided a delightful and appetising lunch. Guests and elementals chatted and communed, exchanging anecdotes and jokes which lightened the atmosphere.

As the dishes and delicacies disappeared, the circle reformed. In the centre of the quartz table, a white mist began to form; swirling in a clockwise direction and changing to blue, then violet. Within the violet mist, a shape was emerging: that of a small, elderly, yet upright man — it was the wizard, Merlin!

He stroked his beard and tidied his windswept cloak. He was rather pleased with his landing technique.

"Well, don't say I've missed lunch! It's always the way with my schedule!"

Smiles and muffled chortles swept around the table and Titania stood; her golden silk dress skimmed her body and her delicate arms stretched out in greeting.

"Merlin, our wise and trusted friend, welcome!"

He bowed and twizzled, completing three circles, then half-tiptoed, half-glided towards Titania. Oberon touched the table to provide an invisible rail, lest he overstepped the edge. Merlin clasped Titania's hands and kissed them lightly.

"Gracious Titania, how exquisite you are! I am at your service. I bring Light from the Ascended Masters. We have studied the *Akashic Records* of each human soul incarnate on the Earth at this time. We have measured the levels of pollution around the entire globe. It is the optimum time for coordinated action from all our realms. This is the moment in human development that has been foretold!"

A quartz-tipped wand somersaulted into Merlin's left hand. As he deftly traced the infinity symbol, a perfectly-formed globe rose from the centre of the table and hovered, suspended in space. Strobes of light penetrated its surface. Like an intelligent, living encyclopaedia, the globe portrayed the Earth's significant events: from its miraculous beginnings until the present moment, from dark conflicts and oppression to the light of scientific discoveries and artistic creations. All were represented in this holographic form. The causes and effects were relayed to all those present.

All activity then subsided and the globe was bathed in the yellow, intellectual ray, the blue ray of true self-expression and the violet ray of insight and spiritual unfoldment. King Oberon stood and spoke for the entire gathering.

"We are amazed and awed by your methods of instruction, Merlin. Now we understand the true significance of this moment, we shall work together to raise the vibrations of this sacred place. Let light refreshments be served before we set to work."

Merlin's eyes twinkled and the assembly showed their appreciation; they clapped and cheered as he was escorted to the delicious buffet. It was at this point that Merlin espied three round faces. They were resting on the lower boughs of the ancient oak, their eyes wide with enchantment. Merlin took a colourful dish of fruit, holding it out towards them in greeting.

"Hello there, young ones. Would you like to try these? I'm Merlin, and you are?"

"Lily,"

"Tom," and

"Megan", they replied, each tasting ripe forest fruits: wild raspberries, strawberries and blueberries, the juice staining their fingers and lips.

"I know that it is almost time for you to return home," smiled Merlin. "I wonder if you would like to help us in the task we are undertaking?"

"Oh, yes!" said Lily. "Of course we would!"

"What would we need to do?" asked Megan.

"Each of you is blessed with a spiritual gift. Yours, Lily, is *clairsentience*. You, Tom, have *clairaudience*, and Megan, you have been given the gift of *clairvoyance*. These gifts will help you to achieve certain things. We shall meet again soon to discuss our project. In the meantime, look after yourselves. All will become clear."

With that, Merlin's wand flew into his left hand and, as he moved it through the air, sparks of light fell onto the children. They seemed to drift into a light sleep, a sleep of forgetfulness. It cleared their conscious minds of the astonishing events that had occurred in the forest.

Aine appeared by Merlin's side and the scent of lavender filled the air. She knelt down and placed a healing balm in Lily's hand and touched each child on the forehead. She stood and smiled at Merlin, linking his arm as they returned to the gathering.

..."Now do you understand what happened that day?" Merlin asked the children, who were looking rather stunned.

"Yes, we do *now*!" said Tom, straightening up and looking somewhat relieved that there was an explanation for the unusual experiences he'd been having lately. "And there's more for us to do, isn't there?"

"Some of those Beings you have already met are here now to ask if you can assist in something of great importance. Let's go through to the glade once more.

Michel led the way. As they approached a bower within the forest, four exquisitely dressed female forms were relaxing around a crystal-blue pool. Dragonflies and butterflies flitted from one leaf to another, landing on clusters of tiny flowers that adorned the outer edges. They were sitting on low, sculpted seats made of bark and lined with moss and petals, their tiny feet dipped in and out of dew-filled flower heads.

The Goddess Aine rose from her seat and introduced herself. Lily recognised her immediately and gave her a radiant smile.

"Good day to you, sweet children. My name is Aine and I'm delighted to see you all again." She reached up to kiss each one. "Do come through and sit with us. I'm going to be working closely with your Aunt Bella to make up some healing and protective infusions. If you would like to assist, Lily, I should be very pleased."

"Oh yes, I've been practising with different herbs," Lily told her.

The Moon Goddess, Rhiannon, introduced herself. She glowed with an incandescent light. Her moonstone, set at the heart, showed a constant flux of colour and activity relayed from Earth. "*Croeso*! I am Rhiannon and I am delighted to meet you."

They touched her delicate hands and immediately felt enveloped in her love.

"I should appreciate your help, Megan, in preparing some crystals for your father who will need them shortly."

Megan was thrilled to be asked. She wanted to learn more about the properties of crystals and where they were mined.

Queen Mab, delicate and wise, introduced herself next. "I am enchanted to meet three beautiful Earth-children," she announced, looking at each one with great affection. *She was the one responsible for assisting the incoming and outgoing souls to find their rightful place,* thought Megan. Queen Mab touched each child lightly on the crown and they felt at ease. "Tom, I wonder if you would help me with my carriage and horses. The steering will come in useful later when you visit your Uncle Jean-Paul," she said, looking directly into his eyes.

Tom had always liked horses but had never found the time to go riding so he accepted the offer, happy to be getting some expert tuition.

The Sun Goddess, Brigit, was waiting to meet these wide-eyed children. "I'm Brigit and I help to regulate the seasons and the harvest. I try to encourage Humankind to eat nutritious foods but don't always succeed," she laughed. "How are you?"

"Very well, thank you," they replied, feeling very much as if they belonged here.

Brigit continued, "I shall be helping your mother and your aunt and I should like you to meet someone very special." She gestured to the bushes on her right where a little boy of about six came skipping through the grass. Brigit introduced him.

"This is Reuben. Say hello to three new friends, Reuben. I'm sure you will be able to play with them later," she said encouragingly.

"Hello Reuben." Lily smiled and knelt down beside him to chat. Tom and Megan said hello too and asked what he had been doing. The Worthington children were thrilled to see such a gorgeous, chubby little boy with a shock of blond curls. He looked just like a cherub. Lily asked Brigit who he belonged to and she explained that Reuben had been staying in the Elemental Realms for a little while, until he is called back into an Earth-family.

"You will all experience something important very soon and you will then understand what I have just told you."

"So," Michel asked them, "do you feel comfortable with your stay here, before returning to *Béziers?*"

The children were unanimous in their response.

17

Time Travel

The year was 1209 Anno Domini. *Béziers* was a thriving city and Roman Catholics lived peacefully alongside another religious group known as the Cathars. There were two levels of devotees: the numerous *believers* and the fewer *pure ones*, who pledged their lives to simplicity, frugality and purity. The *pure ones* gave up their worldly goods and wore black or blue robes, devoting their lives to prayer and good works. Local noblemen also gave their support to these honourable people.

But unease was quickly filtering through to this area as news arrived that a crusading army was making its way down to the *Languedoc* region. *Pierre de Castelnau*, the Pope's legate, had gone to meet *Count Raymond VI of Toulouse*, to excommunicate him as an *abettor* of heresy. After an argument, the monk was murdered whilst on his way to Rome. The Pope, Innocent III, used this event to crush the growing numbers of Cathars. He ordered a crusade against them and enlisted the help of the King of France, Philip Augustus. The King allowed some of his barons to lead the crusade; *Simon de Montfort* and *Bouchard de Marly* were chosen. So began twenty years of war against the Cathars and their supporters in the *Languedoc*; this was known as The *Albigensian* War.

Three members of the inner-sanctum of Cathars in *Béziers* at this time were Christabelle, Henri and Jacques. They helped to feed the poor and prayed for the souls of those who were lost to the Light. The Catholics were intrigued that a woman could hold the position of priestess but all three had earned the respect and approval of those who could discern God's work in action on the earth.

It was a hot July day when the Pope's officials gave the Catholics of *Béziers* an opportunity to leave the city safely and the Cathars were told to recant or die. Christabelle gathered a group of priests together to pray. They realised the enormity of the situation and were weighted with a deep responsibility to maintain the integrity of their faith.

As the new dawn broke, this dedicated band of brothers and sisters made their way through the city, blessing and reassuring Cathars and Catholics alike, urging them to be strong. Mothers packed loaves of bread, chunks of cheese and jugs of mead in panniers or pieces of cloth. They hugged their babies. Fathers took hold of their young and made their way to the churches and city walls. The air was thick with the promise of courage and martyrdom.

The early morning mist began to recede, revealing a vast army of six thousand men making their relentless journey towards *Béziers*. They included many Bishops, the *Duc de Bourgogne*, the *Comtes de Nevers, d'Auxerre and du Genevois* amongst others.

Béziers looked spectacular in the morning sunlight, its raised ramparts and magnificent Cathedral of *Saint-Nazaire* overlooking the glistening river Orb. From the tenth to the twelfth century, it was ruled by the *Counts of Carcassonne*: *Raimond-Rogers, Peter-Raimond* and his son, *Roger.*

Roger died childless and *Béziers* went to his sister, *Ermengard* and her husband, *Raimond-Bertrand Trençavel.* They ruled until the day of the siege, July 22nd, 1209.

A leader of the army, *Arnaud Amaury*, gave a final warning and then his cry went out:

"Kill them all! God will know His own."

Men, women and children were gathered at the fortified walls; horses charged and men wielding swords mutilated everyone within range. The slaughter was horrific; the citizens were defenceless. Yet they showed great courage; the Catholics standing shoulder-to-shoulder beside their fellow countrymen. *Simon de Montfort* led the army in the storming of the defences.

Christabelle, Henri and Jacques were kneeling at the altar of *l'Église de la Madeleine* when members of the King's army entered. Thousands had taken refuge there that day. The irony was that it was the Feast of Mary Magdalene, a day for celebration. The unbearably high-pitched shrieks of children filled the air and the groans of dying men and women tugged at the hearts of Christabelle and her friends. They were encircled around a Sacred Rosary made of wood and semi-precious stones, praying for mercy and the benediction of souls now departing the earth. There was an intense need for this relic, and the sanctity that it represented, to be saved.

It was at this point that something extraordinary occurred.

Three children, in unusual clothing, entered the church through a side door in the nave. They instinctively crouched down and began to crawl along the transept to avoid breathing in the stagnant, curdled air. The three adults at the altar seemed bathed in a protective light. One dark-haired girl carried crystals blessed by Christ and a younger girl carried herbal infusions for protection. A slim, sensitive boy carried candles and, showing great courage, led the way along the narrow aisle. The children recognised the inner essence of the three adults, though their outer form was changed. They knew, from their conversations with Merlin, what they had to do.

The church was packed and chaotic, bodies strewn over the pews as more soldiers elbowed their way in through the main door. They were intent on destroying all life. Megan stood bravely behind Jacques and passed him a handful of radiant crystals. He placed them carefully on a niche in the thick stone wall. Lily gave Christabelle the perfumed infusions and told her to drink and pass the vials to the next person whilst Tom kept watch, unable to take his eyes off the devastating commotion. With a signal from Megan, they led the group to the safety of the waiting carriage outside the church.

Queen Mab had complete faith in her charges and, when all were safely seated within her celestial coach, Tom took the reins and drove them through to the Higher Realms where time and space had no meaning. She introduced the adults to the children.

"Thank you for your help," Jacques said gratefully, "without you we would have perished."

"The vial of liquid tasted like ambrosia and seemed to render us invisible," Christabelle told them in amazement.

"That's exactly what we hoped when we saw the terrible trouble people were in," said Megan. "What will happen to all those poor souls we've left behind?"

"Try not to worry unduly, Megan, there is only so much we can do regarding the past. But you have all set in motion something amazing that will benefit all those people. And the wonderful thing is that you will one day be shown just how much you have helped them," Queen Mab reassured her.

"And Tom has learned to steer the carriage very adeptly," Queen Mab acknowledged, turning to Tom with a look of approval, "and it won't be long before Reuben will be taking the reins."

Reuben, the young spirit-child, giggled and tried to hide behind Tom's shoulder. Bella thought that she had never seen such a beautiful boy.

Queen Mab continued, "There is much work for me to do back there when you reach your destination."

"Where are we going?" Lily asked.

"We shall journey through time, now that you are all safe, back to the twenty-first century."

Laura had been watching these events unfold on a screen set before her in the fifth dimension. She was removed from, yet very much affected by, the whole disastrous episode. She was horrified at the total disregard for human life and the appalling suffering meted out in the name of religion. When she saw her three children in such dreadful danger, her fingers spread across her lips as she stifled a scream. Her relief on their escape was palpable. Yet the history of France, and the world, was one power struggle after another. Mankind didn't seem to learn from past experience. She realised that she had been holding the Light for the development of the souls of Bella, Jean-Paul, Steve and their children as they progressed through other lifetimes. Now they had all reached a place where they could help with the healing of the earth. She was so proud of them all and thrilled that they had all chosen to be together, once more, for the benefit of others. For the moment, her *Karma* was inextricably linked to theirs.

The whole family found themselves together with Merlin and Michel. They looked the same as when they had dressed very early that morning, but in all other respects they were transformed. Wise Merlin greeted them kindly:

"Welcome to the Elemental Realms. Mother Nature will help you to restore your equilibrium. You have all done well. Now prepare yourselves for the journey home."

They formed a circle, it was what they did, and everyone began to feel a build-up of energy, as if they were about to go through some kind of transition. They became acutely aware of each molecule vibrating in their body. And the vibrations became stronger and stronger until there was no resistance. Their present situations began to fade from their awareness and they found themselves travelling at great speed through space and time.

It was a very wet morning on the Square in *Béziers* as four adults and three children found themselves standing in a square- formation and with a slight feeling of disorientation. Laura looked at her watch; it was six minutes past five. They walked towards each other. Each had experienced fundamental changes which would colour the rest of their lives. They gave each other a hug, oblivious to the early morning market traders beginning to stock their stalls. Bella noticed that she was holding a Rosary and a thread of inner-knowing passed through her, subtle yet dynamic, *the work has only just begun.*

Minerve

18

Work and Play

Jean-Paul was looking at each member of his extended family, in awe of their composure and bravery as they stood on Magdalene Square in *Béziers*. He was totally aware that they had all experienced, first-hand, the suffering of those who had lived here centuries before. Past lives were exactly that, a part of our past, our spiritual heritage, and threads from the past could still pull on our hearts and influence our preferences, our choices, even the way we think, he realised.

"Are you alright?" Bella asked him, slipping her hand into his.

"*Mais oui...*" he said, looking a little unsure. "Yes, Bella, are you?"

"Yes...I think so. We've just gone through something pretty amazing, haven't we? I can hardly believe it!"

"It's true, Aunt Bella!" Lily piped up. "We've been back to the time of the Cathars and I knew you then as well, and we all escaped...and you've got those beads in your hand that you had at the altar!" she said, pointing to the Rosary.

"Let's go and find somewhere to sit and have breakfast and just get our bearings," Steve suggested. He had one arm around Laura and the other around Megan. *Goodness*, he remembered, *there was a time very recently when I thought I'd lost them...lost everything*!

Tom and Megan were sharing snippets of their most recent adventure in hushed tones. It had become a bit of a habit until they realised that the others were very much in on this one too! They didn't have to protect Lily anymore; they could speak freely if they wanted to.

The sky was clearing and everywhere felt fresher after the storm. After breakfast and a relaxing walk by the *Canal du Midi*, the family strolled back to their car. Jean-Paul suggested they could visit *Minerve* to say a prayer and place crystals on a site to commemorate the Cathars. They would then drive to nearby *Carcassonne* to their *chambre d'hôte*, where they could relax. This was agreeable to everyone. Megan, Tom and Lily were thrilled that they were going to stay somewhere that had a pool.

When they arrived in *Minerve,* the children were especially awed by the position of this ancient Roman site. It was still quite inaccessible, with a narrow bridge leading into the town. They wandered the narrow streets, finding references to the town's history in tiny shops, museums and *l'Église St-Nazaire.*

They learned that it was the strongest fortified castle at the time and lay in the foothills of the *Cevennes.* Its landscape was sculpted by two rivers: the *Cesse* and the *Brian*. It was the town where many Cathars took refuge after the sacking of *Béziers. Simon de Montfort* led the ten-week siege a year later. His men set up four huge catapults: three to attack the fortifications and one to cut off the water supply. Viscount *Guilhem de Minerve* and 200 men tried to resist but, with no water, they were

162

eventually forced to surrender. About 180 *pure ones* were burned when they refused to recant.

A plaque marked the site of the Cathar murders. Here, the family of seven stood, each touching the Sacred Rosary as Laura led the prayers. Lily lit her smudge to cleanse the area and offer a protective perfume. It was Lily who asked a very pertinent question. "What does the Rosary do, Aunt Bella?"

"That's such a good question, Lily," she began. "I've been asking myself the same thing since you mentioned it earlier. You know, many people from various religions use beads when they pray. Catholics use a rosary, Buddhists use prayer beads and Hindus wear and use a mala. They pass the beads through their fingers as they say special prayers or chant. The beads help them to focus their minds so that they can reach something beyond themselves, beyond their everyday concerns. This reverence, or honour, begins to rest in the beads and makes the spiritual more accessible. Do you understand?"

"I think so," Lily responded.

Everyone had been listening and Tom added his thoughts, "You mean the beads help people to go beyond their physical lives and experience their spirituality."

"That is exactly what I mean, Tom." Bella thought that there was greater significance in what he had said and she was trying to grasp it. *What if we exist in other realms as well as the earthly one, all at the same time*? she pondered. *What if we are multi-dimensional beings?*

This visit to Minerve gave the family, especially the children, an opportunity to integrate the two worlds they had straddled — the past and the present, the spiritual and the temporal. They strolled back across to the other side of the bridge and the next part of their journey.

The guest house stood atop a wooded hillside overlooking the magical fortress that was the old *cité* of *Carcassonne.* The manager came out to meet them as they parked on the gravel drive.

"Bonjour tout le monde. Bienvenue à Carcassonne. Do you need any help with your bags?" he asked.

"Oh, no thank you," Steve replied. "Can you recommend anywhere for lunch?"

"If a salad is all right, we could serve one here by the pool?"

"That would be perfect. We've been on the road since very early morning."

"Well, come along in. My wife will give you the keys and show you the rooms."

They carried their holdalls into the foyer. It looked very pleasant, clean and airy with some lovely pieces of French farmhouse furniture. They heard the brisk click of high heels across the stone floor and Mme Latour appeared at their side, smiling warmly. She was petite with a dark, neat bob and wearing plum-red lipstick.

"Hello, I'm *Madame Latour*, I hope you've had a good journey."

The family told her their names and Steve signed the residents' book. She gave them three keys and, in her efficient manner, led the way up to the first floor.

"I hope you'll be very comfortable here. Please ask if there's *autre chose.* I'll serve lunch by the pool in an hour. Let me know, when you come down, if you'd like aperitifs."

The rooms were beautiful, set side by side along the front of the house. They were light and unexpectedly modern, with thick-pile rugs on polished oak floors. The cotton bed linen was lightly patterned and beautifully pressed, and not a trace of flowery wallpaper in sight. Lily was thrilled that there were duvets, even in the summer she liked the weight of a duvet to snuggle under. Megan and Lily could see the pool from their side window. They had twin beds and, this time, it was Megan's turn to choose the one she preferred.

After getting washed and changed, the children were wearing their swimming costumes under their shorts and t-shirts. The pool looked very inviting; its sparkling water was tinged blue from the tiny royal-blue tiles which covered the interior walls, and a beautiful mosaic dolphin beckoned playtime to the children. At the moment, there were no other visitors. The recliners were arranged around the edge, with several circular tables and chairs standing on a large terrace at one end.

They made themselves comfortable around the pool, along with suncreams of various factors, sun-hats, flip-flops, books and other paraphernalia, ready for an undisturbed afternoon of lounging and fun. *Monsieur Latour* arrived with a tray of drinks. He apologised for serving them in a glass-substitute but it was one of their safety rules.

"Very sensible," Jean-Paul concurred. "It's too late when a nasty accident happens."

After lunch had settled, the children jumped into the pool with Steve and Jean-Paul. They had swimming races, underwater races and played water volleyball. Laura and Bella lay on their sunbeds, reading and occasionally chatting.

"We've completed the first triangle of energy-work now. It's been a tremendous learning curve," Bella told her sister.

"Yes, and we're in the right place to begin the second phase, the old *cité* of *Carcassonne*."

"I think the most difficult part is over, don't you? The Rosary that you've brought back is going to be very effective in the healing work. Tell me, Bella, how *did* you come to have it?"

Bella stretched out and closed her eyes and, in a reflective voice, she recounted a scene from the distant past. "I remember walking down towards the church where crowds were gathering, hoping for protection from the King's men. It was chaotic and terrifying. There was the choking smell of burning as smoke drifted, obliterating some of the scenes of carnage. As a patch of the smog cleared, I could see a dark-robed, charismatic man, standing in the midst of a gathering group of horrified townsfolk. His voice was rich and melodious as he chanted prayers, holding a beautiful circlet of beads that seemed to mesmerise everyone. At that moment, the priest...or...prior looked up and caught my gaze. He had the kindest eyes and seemed totally becalmed and confident. Then he spoke in Occitan, my own language, *'Take this, a Sacred Rosary from the Holy Mother. She knows that you have need of it.'*

I was astonished, yet deeply moved, that he should entrust this blessed gift to me. There was no time to delay so I simply thanked him, took it, and rushed into the side-door of the church."

"How extraordinary!" Laura half-whispered to herself as Bella blinked open her eyes into the vibrant sunlight.

"I wonder if we should keep it, Laura, or will we need to hand it over to someone?"

"I know that we need to use it soon. Maybe it should then go to the head of a church."

"You mean the Pope?" Bella suggested.

"Perhaps, but what would he actually do with it? Surely it needs to be in the hands of those who are active in this new healing work."

"It might be wisest to ask Michel Ange," Bella concluded.

Steve's phone rang; his latest choice was Bob Dylan's "Blowing in the Wind". Laura thought Steve would have been a beach-bum if he'd been around in the sixties — one of those relaxed American professors setting up scientific experiments on the beach with lanterns and wooden coracles to represent the movement of heavenly bodies. As it was, she wasn't a fan of Bob Dylan, so Laura answered the phone. It was Michel Ange. What serendipity! How did he *do* that? He asked Laura how things were going. She told him about the Rosary. He sounded impressed and thought that they should use it over the next few days. How were they fixed to meet the Pope at the Palace in Avignon on Sunday?

When she had found her voice, she told him that they would be honoured. Michel suggested that they meet up at the hotel in *St Guilhem–le-Désert* on Saturday evening for dinner. It would be a suitable stop over for their Sunday morning appointment. Laura said that she would discuss it with everyone but that she was sure this would be perfect and that she would phone to confirm.

When Steve and Jean-Paul came over to collect their towels, Laura told them the amazing news. They decided to tell the children over dinner. In the meantime, their offspring were enjoying their freedom and the glorious weather.

Le Cité – Carcassonne

Le Château Comtal

19

Murmurings of Mummies

The Worthington family and the Lefèvres went indoors late afternoon to have an hour's rest and to shower and change, ready for dinner in the *cité*. It was only a kilometre walk downhill so they set off at seven. The *cité* looked spectacular, bathed in the pink light of early evening.

As they neared one of the gateways, Jean-Paul gave the family a précis of its history.

"The fortified nucleus of the *cité*, built on the east bank of the Aude, is the *Château Comtal*. Its double curtain of fortified walls contains 24 towers on the inner ramparts and 14 towers on the outer ones. It stood as a veritable fairytale castle, seemingly impregnable. For four hundred years it was the capital of the region, linking Toulouse with the Mediterranean.

Then, on August 1st, 1209, the Cathar Crusade reached these daunting fortifications. *Raimond-Roger Trençeval*, the Viscount of *Carcassonne*, tried to resist the siege but he did not want the same thing to happen to his city as had happened in *Béziers*. So, when water ran out, he surrendered himself and was taken prisoner. *Simon de Montfort* was given his position. Everyone was expelled from the city. It became one of the first European sites of the Papal Inquisition, an ongoing brutal scourge to rid the land of *heretics.*"

"I've heard of the Spanish Inquisition," Tom said, "and that was all to do with torture and murder, to try to get people to think the same things that the rulers thought and believed in."

"Yes, Tom, that pretty much describes what happened here."

"It looks amazing — and huge!" Megan commented, more interested in taking out her camera than thinking about past horrors.

"You're right, Megan," Jean-Paul agreed. "It's the largest fortress in Europe and has been a UNESCO World Heritage site since 1997."

"Have a good look at the main entrance, the *Porte Narbonnaise*, when we go through," Bella told them. "Ten points for spotting the feature."

They were keen, now, to have a really good look for anything especially interesting.

"There are two enormous towers!" Tom told Bella.

"Yes," she agreed. "Ten points to you, Tom."

"There are arrow slits to protect the gateway," Megan added.

"Yes," repeated Bella. "Ten points to you, Megan."

"Look there!" Lily pointed. "Right in the middle of the archway; it's a statue of Mother Mary!"

"Well done, Lily. To think it's been there since the thirteenth century, the time that we went back to," she said quietly, looking from one to the other.

The family stood underneath this memorial for a moment. Laura wondered who had carved it and raised it into position, to gaze down on every person who came through the gateway.

"Ten points for you, Lily," Jean-Paul confirmed, "and to anyone else who spots something of interest during the evening."

Megan stepped back a few paces to take a photo, then zoomed in for a close-up. She absolutely loved her new camera.

They headed towards the centre of the *cité*, which was very busy with throngs of people enjoying the unique atmosphere. Megan began to feel disorientated and stumbled off the kerb. Through the gaps between people wandering past her, she could see women, men and children clawing at the stonework. Their faces were contorted with horror, their mouths fixed in a shriek of despair.

Tom rushed over to Megan and whispered, "Are you all right?"

"It's happening again, Tom!" she gasped.

"I know. I can hear the screams and sobbing coming from the walls! What shall we do?"

"Nothing at the moment; it's too late. We'll have to come back tomorrow when we're feeling fresher and the light is fading fast now."

"Do people actually live here?" Lily was asking her uncle, completely unaware of the drama unfolding behind her. They were making their way, two-abreast, along the cobbled street.

"Yes, they do. There are about a 150 residents running restaurants, hotels, gift shops and museums. There's also a school and a post office. Children still learn the old language, the *Langue d'Oc*, which is where the name of the region comes from, of course."

"Otherwise, it would be like a ghost town when the visitors have gone," Megan added knowingly as she and Tom caught them up.

"Who speaks the *Langue d'Oc* these days?" Tom asked.

"Probably a few million people still, especially the older generations. It's a way of keeping it alive or it would simply disappear. It's a part of the cultural heritage around here," Bella clarified. "I've been taking a part-time language course at the college where I teach for the past few years. It's the same as any other language, it takes many years to become fluent, unless you study it from when you're young. You're all doing brilliantly with your French," she complimented them.

The children marvelled at the magnificent towers and buildings and enjoyed looking in gift shops. They came to a restaurant that looked inviting and went inside for their evening meal. Later, they walked back to the *chambre d'hôte*.

After a long sleep and a late, leisurely breakfast on the terrace, everyone returned to their rooms to pack. Steve settled the bill, the least he could do to balance the incredible hospitality of his sister-in-law and her husband. They thanked the owners for their comfortable stay and promised to return.

The weather seemed settled again as they drove down to the car park opposite the main entrance to the *cité.* There was a carousel for young children who were enjoying rides whilst their parents waved.

"Can we have an ice cream when we come across a kiosk?" Lily asked anyone who was listening.

"Yes," Laura said, "but let's do what we came to do first."

"What did we come to do?" Lily asked.

"Lily, the history of this place isn't good," Megan told her.

"What happened here, then?"

"It's not very pleasant," Jean-Paul began. "The *cité* came under siege. It wasn't burned, but when the lands and its fortress had been taken, the Pope ordered an Inquisition to keep the locals in check and it was based here."

"What happened to the people here?" Lily persisted.

It was Megan who answered. "It was the Cathars again — and those who supported them. They were tortured, starved and bricked up inside the walls if they didn't recant."

"That is horrible! How do you know that?"

"I saw it. Last night, as we walked through the streets, I could see what had gone on here all those years ago. And Tom *heard* it, didn't you?"

"Why didn't you say something?" Laura asked them both.

"We didn't want to spoil the evening and I have seen such horrors in recent weeks that I just wanted to forget it. It doesn't make it any easier but I now understand that we can help in some way and, when we have helped, the images go away." Megan explained.

"We've all learned something very valuable in the last few days," Steve said. "We've seen, and experienced, both sides of the coin: Good and Evil. We know that the world is changing. The Light is dissolving the Darkness as long as people like us are willing to help. We have all grown so much in the past few weeks and, as we become whole, so does the world."

"Will you two take us to the places that you know need healing?" Laura asked Megan and Tom.

"Yes, we'll be glad to," Megan answered for both of them.

"I think it's an opportunity to use our double-terminated crystals," Laura suggested. "We can pray and use them to direct energy at the walls that have consumed people."

"I can waft my smudge to protect us and clear the air," Lily added.

Megan and Tom led the way to places they knew people had suffered and died. These included the parts of the walls where, yesterday, they had seen and heard the horror of the past.

They were working together as a team, just as Merlin had known they would.

They had lunch in the *cité*, eating and drinking were very grounding; everyone now felt more balanced and at ease. It was time to get on the road, travelling south-east back to *St-Paul-de-Fenouillet*. They called at an open-air market in the village of *Tuchan* to buy fresh ingredients for the next few days and then headed home, knowing that their work in *Carcassonne* was complete.

20

Preparations and Misgivings

It was good to get home. Shutters and windows were flung open all over the house and the whole family enjoyed a cup of tea and a slice of *tarte aux fruits* on the terrace. The children emptied their holdalls before changing into shorts and t-shirts to spend time in the garden. The automatic sprinklers would soon come on and they still loved diving in and out of them.

That evening, Megan and Lily went upstairs to work on their homemade presents for Tom's birthday. Tom went up to play his violin, with strict instructions not to disturb the girls. Steve and Jean-Paul had a game of chess whilst Bella and her sister tidied up and made some fresh coffee. Everybody welcomed the opportunity to relax and enjoy themselves after the busy and tiring few days. However, there was a growing feeling amongst the adults that something else, possibly more sinister, was coming their way.

"So, tomorrow's the last work day for all of us," Bella looked over at her sister. "Do you think everything will go well?"

"Let's hope so. We're going to visit *Montségur and Peyrepertuse*, aren't we?"

Bella nodded. "I wonder what we'll find there?" she asked.

"Hopefully, nothing like you found in *Béziers*," Laura commented. "Though, you all did amazingly well. You were so brave."

"It's interesting that it was the children who helped us escape. I shudder to think what else could have happened!" Bella said.

"I know; they're fantastic!"

"Let's take our coffee through and have a look at the book that Merlin gave to Steve," Bella suggested, squeezing Laura's arm.

Laura opened it at the chapter on Twin Flames and Soul Mates. She explained to her sister the difference between these and illustrated this with the example of her own life.

"Steve is my Soul Mate, Bella. I realised this just before we came to France. We belong to the same soul group and, therefore, share a common bond and the same impetus for growth. We recognise each other's inner spirit."

"Whilst you were in a previous incarnation, in *Béziers,* I was taken up into the Higher Realms. I oversaw your experiences, helping energetically when I could. But I also had a meeting with my Twin Flame."

"Who was that?" Bella asked, intrigued.

"It's Angel Michael. I'm going to tell you something that I have never told anyone," Laura confided. "During my teens, occasionally, just when I was in that state between sleeping and waking, I would hear the words, '*kiss me*'. I never knew where the words came from. They didn't worry me; I wasn't even *that* curious. But they were gentle and loving words.

When Steve and I first got married, I would sometimes wake and call Steve, *Michael*. It was just one of those things. Steve wasn't put out about it and he never asked if I'd had a boyfriend of that name.

One evening, just before bedtime about five years ago, I was meditating in my bedroom. I was in that still, silent place within my own being. My mind was absolutely quiet when I heard those beautiful words once more, '*kiss me'.*

I asked, '*Who is it?*' And the response came, '*I am your Beloved. At last you are awake to me. I have waited aeons of time for this moment. When your life is over, we will go forward together.*'

Then I felt his sublime energy descend into mine. From that time, I felt somehow more whole. My energy changed and I know that these words were the Truth. When I leave this Earth, I shall go to him."

"That is such a beautiful thing to happen," Bella told her sister and they hugged each other. "Does Steve know?"

"No. I don't think he ever will, Bella. This makes no difference to how I feel about Steve. I would never give him any cause to think that he was somehow second best. It's better this way."

"Has Michael ever contacted you again?"

"No, not until I actually saw him when I was taken up into a higher dimension. He is so beautiful and I felt an overwhelming and inexplicably deep love for him. I don't think he will contact me again. I need to live my own life here and do the best I can."

"You are so blessed," Bella told her sister.

"And so are you, Bella."

Jean-Paul and Steve came in from the terrace. Steve was looking quite smug; he had won this game. The children came down to say goodnight as Jean-Paul got the map out and brought it into the sitting room.

"Any cake left, Aunt Bella?" Tom asked cheekily as he popped his head round the door.

"It's all gone! But there are biscuits in the larder and make yourselves some hot chocolate to take up to bed if you want to," she told them.

There was a bit of a scuffle behind the door and a vote for a feast in Tom's room. Lily came through to kiss them goodnight before going upstairs.

Jean-Paul was studying the map. "Let me show you where we're going tomorrow. They're the other two points on the triangle. If we go to the furthest first, that's *Montségur*, then we can visit *Peyrepertuse* on our way back. Is that OK with everyone?"

"Yes, that sounds good," Laura said. "Will you bring the Rosary, Bella?"

"Definitely!"

"What do you know about *Montségur*, Jean-Paul?" Steve asked.

"It's one of the most inaccessible sites. The castle is perched on a huge, craggy, granite cliff. The route from the car park is steep and treacherous in bad weather."

"What's the forecast for tomorrow?" Bella asked her husband. "The wind may be getting up and there are scattered showers forecast. We've had mainly settled weather for so long now; it's inevitable that we'll get a few thundery downpours."

"Does it have to be *Montségur* that we go to?" Laura asked.

"We did choose the sites using our intuition, didn't we?" Bella reminded her.

"This castle is quite significant," Jean-Paul continued. "It was here that the final siege of the Cathar Crusade took place. It's said that ten thousand men came to lay siege to the castle in 1243. In the spring of the following year, ten months later, *Pierre-Roger de Mirepoix* surrendered, but the fate of the Cathars was sealed. They chose to die as martyrs rather than renounce their faith."

"The site itself is very ancient, and the castle remains are not the ones that stood at the time of the Cathar Crusade. Nevertheless, it is the actual site of the siege and is a memorial to those who died," Bella explained.

Steve looked at Bella. "It seems that we're destined to visit this place in the morning."

"Yes, then *Peyrepertuse*," she said. "It's the final phase."

Jean-Paul's weather forecast was spot on. The wind picked up in the night. The trees were rustling, branches creaking and there was the occasional rattle of a door or chimney-pot. It was easy to believe that autumn was making its claim. The children slept soundly but the adults were restless, perhaps remembering what Steve had told them about the Dark Forces. Hadn't Merlin said there could be a final challenge?

Steve got up and went to the bathroom. He splashed his face with cold water and looked at his reflection. What more could he do than do his best? What more did God want from him?

You have my Constancy, Devotion and Love.
I need nothing more from you.
I live in thee, and thou in Me. We are as one.
Remember these things.

Steve got into bed and drifted back to sleep.

It was Friday morning and there were a few clouds in the sky but the wind had subsided. Things always seemed better in the morning.

They were all sitting around the kitchen table when Jean-Paul had an idea. "How do you feel about a spot of climbing today, Megan?"

Steve looked startled but waited for Megan to respond.

"The cliff face at *Montségur* would be great for a challenge," her uncle added.

"Wow! That would be fantastic!" Megan replied, jumping up and down with excitement. She'd been hoping to go climbing with her uncle since they went to the *Cirque de Navacelles.* "I'll get my climbing gear on when I've finished breakfast."

Steve was stunned. Hadn't Jean-Paul said, himself, the night before that the cliff path could be treacherous? And now the *cliff face*! What was he thinking?

"I'll come along too," Steve said rather flatly, looking askance at his brother-in-law.

Laura felt a strange sense of *déjà-vu*. She felt unable to protest yet there was a disconcerting sense of unease.

They finished breakfast in silence, tidied the kitchen, then went to pack their rucksacks for the day ahead. Bella and Laura sorted some drinks and a packed lunch.

Jean-Paul went down to the *sous-sol* to collect suitable equipment, bearing in mind their difference in weights and that Megan needed to wear a harness. He had a collection of hats that his students borrowed and extra cagoules. Steve had brought his climbing shoes and Megan had brought all her gear: pink/grey shoes, cerise three-quarter trousers, a dark grey hoody and her smart new pair of climbing gloves from *Millau.*

Megan was so excited when she went to get changed. Her enthusiasm was contagious and Tom said he would take some photos of them when they set off up the cliff. Lily was quickly putting on her trainers and she was going to take her cagoule; the weather didn't look too promising.

Within an hour, they were all set and the minibus was loaded. The children chatted animatedly in the back. Steve was looking at the map and Jean-Paul was concentrating on the narrow roads; Fridays were always busier. Laura and Bella were sitting together companionably, commenting on the scenery and the fact that they would be on their travels again the next day with another overnight stay. They couldn't bring themselves to talk about Sunday; a meeting with the Pope just seemed too surreal.

They were travelling due west along the D117 for about 70 kilometres. This route took in several other castles through *le Pays Cathare: Puilaurens, Quillan and Puivert.* The scenery was spectacular, with wooded hillsides, rivers and gorges. Bella passed the children a drink and then they all had a mint. The taste reminded Steve of his climbs in the Lake District when he always took a bar of Kendal Mint Cake. They were due to go up there in the October half-term. Bella and Jean-Paul were coming over in the minibus and bringing the children's bikes.

Montségur

21

Landscapes and Revelations

As they drove through *Fougax-et-Barrineuf*, they could see the high dome of *Montségur* looming upwards into the darkening sky. It stood at over twelve hundred metres above the *Ariège* landscape, in the foothills of the Pyrenees.

When they arrived, they decided to do some stretches. It would take at least an hour and a half to walk the criss-cross pathway up to the castle and back, whereas the climbers would need several hours for their ascent, if they scrambled up the lower green slopes to where the sheer, weathered rock emerged.

Jean-Paul was leading the climbers, ropes and the *jingling jangly* hardware slung comfortably across his shoulder. Megan followed like a mountain goat, her slight frame hardly seeming to make contact with the boulders and tufted sedge. Tom and Bella were taking photos. Steve moved methodically, his stomach tightening as they reached the dry rock face. The sun was peeping through the clouds, throwing a shaft of light onto the party.

Jean-Paul explained a few things to Megan and made sure that she knew the emergency procedures. They wished each other *bonne chance* and her uncle set off. Steve's stomach knotted.

Bella, Laura, Tom and Lily found the narrow path that led upwards and across the steep cliff. They were in good spirits and ready for something a bit more exacting. Even Lily felt more agile and fit after a summer of outdoor living. Every so often, they stood and looked out onto the landscape, identifying landmarks from the map that Bella was carrying. They were making good progress.

Jean-Paul was expertly selecting hand and foot-holds on the cliff face whilst placing running belays to protect himself should he slip. He had two 60m ropes and was aiming to climb in 40m stretches.

When he reached the first suitable ledge he attached himself to the rock using a fixed belay. Steve had been holding the rope firmly below, concentrating and occasionally glancing at Megan who was standing primed to his left. He knew that she was keen and had great potential. Steve spoke encouragingly to Megan and tied her on. She was to go up next, unclipping her rope from the runners as she climbed before clipping them to the second rope which Steve had tied into. Steve set off slightly behind, so that he could advise her if need-be.

Rain clouds began to gather and the wind started to blow up from nowhere. Bella's team zipped up their cagoules and quickened their pace.

Bella turned to tell the children. "Keep well into the cliff!"

Tom was right behind her, followed by Lily and then Laura. Bella knew that water would render the path slippery and dangerous. There was nothing to hold onto as they walked single-file. Laura had a heavy feeling in the pit of her stomach. How were the climbers getting on?

They had all reached the first ledge, and Jean-Paul had set off, following the same procedures, to the second one. But the weather had deteriorated. It was raining hard, big spots hitting their faces and hands and then pelting into their eyes. It was a hailstorm!

Lily moaned, "I can't see a thing! Can we stop for a bit?"

"Yes!" called Bella, turning again to look at the children. "Secure your hoods. Have you brought gloves?"

"I've got mine in my pocket," Tom told her. He got them out quickly, feeling that his pendant and stone were still there, and zipped them in.

Lily had remembered to bring her gloves too. Bella wished they could have been roped together for the path was very narrow and becoming slippery! As she looked past the children, further down the hillside, Bella thought she saw another person but the size of the figure was quite large and fluid and it seemed to be moving rather too quickly. As it closed in, it appeared to have no more substance than a shadow — a dark, looming shape.

Megan and Steve were locked into the cliff face, trying to protect themselves. It was impossible! Jean-Paul tried to reassure Megan and shouted to them on the ledge that they should all press on. Relentless icy pellets rained down on them like mechanised marbles shooting from the ramparts. Bits of shale began to loosen and slide. Steve knew it was a dangerous situation. Why hadn't he said something earlier? Megan must be terrified!

Then Jean-Paul called to Megan that she should go down! He had created a belay above the pair and secured himself. Megan was relieved that this was still an option. Steve helped her to untie from the stance belay and told her to take up the same position as for an abseil. She placed her feet flat against the rock whilst pushing outwards and downwards; she was on her way! Steve had been in the best position to lower her and do the necessary checks, and he began to breathe again.

Megan reached the ground safely. She was a bit shaken but she had not felt in any real danger. It was the sudden change in the weather which had heightened her awareness of her predicament. She made her way back to their vehicle, which had been left unlocked.

The rain abated and Steve climbed up to the next ledge to join Jean-Paul. They decided to alternate leads, so Jean-Paul swapped his gear over to his brother-in-law. They shook hands and Steve set off with renewed confidence. They were working together: focused, committed, in harmony. Nothing else existed as they scaled the sheer face. It was the brotherhood of the rope.

Meanwhile, Bella had tried to quicken her pace, urging Tom, Lily and Laura to keep up. She hardly dared to look behind her but, when she eventually did so, a gaping, vaporous mass enveloped her. A deep cold shiver wracked her body. Something heavy and odorous lunged into her back and forced her over the edge! She let out a piercing scream that echoed around the hills as she rolled and tumbled down the soggy bank.

Megan glanced up to see if she could spot Tom and Lily on the path but, as she squinted into the light, she saw a person — it looked like Aunt Bella —

falling and rolling downwards towards her! She put her hands over her mouth and then started to run full-pelt.

Laura was aghast! What on earth had happened to Bella? One minute she was steaming ahead and the next, she was disappearing over the edge. Laura studied the spot where Bella left the path but there was no obstruction or disturbance in the earth. It was as if she'd been whisked into the air by some unseen force.

Megan reached Bella quickly and crouched down by her aunt. She gently felt down her limbs and asked if she was in any pain, or indeed if she could *not* feel any part of her body. Bella was bruised and grazed but it appeared nothing was broken and her breathing had become quite steady. Megan used her aunt's mobile to tell her mother the news and told her to continue upwards to meet her dad and Uncle Jean-Paul. It would be far safer if they all came down together; her uncle had ropes.

Megan carefully helped Bella to her feet. She was relieved the hail had stopped. They came down the slope to the car park, Megan leading Bella with encouraging words and a gentle smile.

As the walkers reached the top, Tom and Lily breathed deeply. They were feeling a sense of achievement but upset that their aunt had had such a terrible fall. However, they could now see her walking slowly but steadily, and supported by Megan, back to the car. Laura and her children walked through the castle remains. It was an elongated pentagon, majestically perched and overlooking the beautiful French countryside. Tom and Lily ran to strategic points on the ramparts to see if they could spot the climbers. They were perfectly positioned to witness first Jean-Paul, followed by Steve, appear at the summit.

It was a subdued reunion as Laura recounted the news, though she didn't really know how it had happened. They rested for a moment on some huge boulders and had a quick drink from the warm thermos that Laura had been carrying. They wanted to begin the descent as soon as possible but the whole point of them tackling the steep route to this awesome site was not only to test their courage and skills, but to pray as a family and secrete the powerful crystals. Laura knew that everyone was keen to see how Bella was, but it was too important to be left undone. This was the place where the final siege of the Cathars had taken place all those centuries ago.

"Listen Jean-Paul, we need to place the crystals before going down to Bella, it will only take a few minutes."

"Yes, I understand that, but let's hurry."

Laura took out the velvet pouch from her backpack. She and the children took one crystal each. The power shot through them and they nearly lost their balance. Tom held an aquamarine, pure and brilliant and reflecting the light and the sea. Lily was holding a sphere of quartz that seemed to contain the whole world within its smooth surface. She peered inside and could see the rolling, green hills of the nearby countryside and the craggy outcrop on which they were standing. But what was that coming into view? An army of soldiers on horseback, standards flapping in the wind, a fire blazing, and shrieks and screams…! Lily tore her eyes away from the scene as tears trickled down her rosy cheeks.

"What is it, Lily?" Steve asked, seeing her distress.

"N...nothing Daddy. Where shall we hide these?" she asked, sniffing and wiping her cheeks with her glove.

Laura was holding a piece of deep blue lapis lazuli that reminded her of Egypt and ancient tombs. She told the children to go with her as she searched for a suitable position. She found a chink between two sturdy rocks, within reach of them all.

"Let's place them now and say a silent prayer — whatever comes to mind."

Jean-Paul decided to use the rope for their descent, just in case, and they all walked down the narrow path, the children sandwiched between the adults.

Bella was resting in the minibus after drinking a hot, sweet tea with Megan, who had helped her out of her muddied parka. She was trying to keep her composure, not just because of the fall but because she knew for certain that she had fallen prey to some dark entity that was wandering the hills!

"What happened up there?" Megan asked her aunt.

"*You've* had some very strange experiences these past few weeks, Megan. This morning, I've just had one of my own! It's not something that I ever thought could happen. I don't want to frighten you but I need to tell you that the Darkness is real. I was pushed off that path; I didn't just fall!"

It took a few moments for Megan to absorb this.

"Did you see anything?" Megan asked, her eyes wide with fear.

"Yes, sort of. It was a dark and malevolent shadow that packed an almighty punch! I felt this thud in the middle of my back — and I was over the edge."

"What shall we do? Is there anything we can do to stop it? Will it come back?" Megan was trying to keep calm and to understand the enormity of the situation. *How vast were the Dark Forces? Where did they live? How could you prepare to fight them? Were the others safe?*

"Megan, I haven't got all the answers but I know it happened for a reason. Maybe it was to show us that we need to regroup, stand firm, and use all the knowledge and skills that we've learned since you came over to stay. When the others get here, will you talk to Tom and Lily while I talk to your mum and dad and Jean-Paul? I don't want to worry Lily or any of you unduly."

"Yes, I understand. We'll think of something positive to do, Aunt Bella. How're you feeling now?"

"I'm not too bad. That makes me realise just how serious it could have been. I *was* protected."

Megan tidied up the minibus, because everyone would want to get changed, and she put a comforting blanket around Bella's shoulders, who began to doze while Megan took a book from her hold-all; it was the French version of Paulo Coelho's *The Pilgrimage.*

When Jean-Paul was satisfied that Bella really was all right, they went outside to discuss what could be done, leaving the children to get changed

"Something is very clear to me now," Bella told them. "This really is the final phase, for us and for the powers of Darkness in this area. We must complete the Sacred Triangle, no matter how much we're intimidated. We have got to finish it here!"

"Bravo, Bella!" Jean-Paul said, giving her a gentle hug.

"Let's say a prayer using the Rosary and I'll light some incense on the exact place where the pyre was lit all those years ago," Laura suggested.

"We need to stay focused; remember what Merlin told us," Steve reminded them.

At that point, the children came running from the minibus.

"We've just helped Lily write a verse!" Tom was shouting.

"Mummy! Can we chant it? Can we chant it?" Lily was calling.

"Let me see." As Laura read the words, a tingle went through her. "It's an invocation. We can all chant this together."

The grown-ups read it silently and memorised the words.

"Are we all wearing our pendants?" Megan asked.

Tom put his on and held the aventurine stone in his fist. His dad and uncle then went to put on clean clothes, followed by Laura, who did a bit of tidying up before freshening herself up too.

As they set about their preparations, the sky darkened. There was a sense of being watched. Amorphous shapes began to gather, looming up out of the undergrowth as if from unseen graves. Lily found her smudge, a tightly packed bundle of herbs, and asked her dad to light it. She wafted the sweet-smelling smoke around each person and all around the grassy hillock. Laura placed small branches of artemesia, lavender, blackthorn, sage and fennel above some tinder. Steve lit it and an intoxicating mix of smoke and perfume spiralled upwards. Bella was sitting with the Rosary, seemingly deep in thought, whilst Jean-Paul traced out a circle with rope, making sure the ends were overlapping and secured.

Fronds of icy blackness started to pull at the children's arms and legs as they made their way towards the circle. Tom was pushed and pulled until he stumbled, falling into Megan.

"It's begun!" shouted Steve. "Focus only on the Light right NOW!"

They each pushed through what felt like a wall of impenetrable pressure, thrashing with their fists and kicking out to shake off the grotesque, cloying tendrils.

"HURRY! HURRY! HURRY!" Laura was calling from the inner sanctum. "I'LL HELP YOU! KEEP MOVING!" she shouted.

Bella was striding towards the circle, holding the Rosary tightly and praying aloud, "Our Father, who art in Heaven, Hallowed be Thy name, Thy kingdom come…"

Steve was lurching towards Megan and Jean-Paul was trying to reach Tom. It was like being caught up in a gale-force wind that had turned against the powers of creation. There was a wild roar of aggression that sounded as if it would rip out the beating heart from any living thing that faltered. A low moaning wailed and sighed in turns; the breath of the Beast was getting closer!

Lily, meanwhile, was spinning like a top. She was still holding onto her smudge and had decided the best way up the hill was to keep turning and wafting. Her progress was slow but unimpeded and she was the first person to be pulled over the threshold and into the circle by her mother. Bella was next as both Lily and Laura took one arm and, gently but firmly, pulled her into what was beginning to feel like a nest.

The three stood together, willing encouragement to the four who continued to battle their way upwards. It was useless to shout; they would never be heard in the din that now echoed around them. And they knew better than to let their minds wander down the path of *what ifs*.

"Let's start the chant," Laura said defiantly.

So they stood in a small group and, holding onto the Rosary, they began,

Ring, ring, ring of Light,
Stand our ground
And bless this site,
Prayers and pendants, crystals bright,
Dissolve the Darkness into Light.

Something began to change in the energies around them, sufficient for Steve and Jean-Paul to make a break from the opposing forces.

Tom had been trying to battle through with all of his strength when he had an idea. "Please help me!" he shouted, holding onto his pendant and hoping someone, somewhere, would hear above the cacophony of the groaning wind.

Suddenly, Tom found himself standing inside the circle. The wind had abated and he was feeling calmer. A large crow came swooping and cawing through the air. It landed effortlessly on his forearm. The weight of the bird was quite something! Tom looked at it in disbelief.

"You called?" it seemed to ask him.

"Yes, I needed some help," Tom replied, quite glad now that the others were busy chanting.

"Well, I came, didn't I?" the bird asked indignantly, his beak lightly preening a few tufts of wing feathers. Tom realised that the bird wasn't *actually* speaking, they were communicating telepathically!

"Yes, but, *who* are you?" Tom asked, not quite believing that he'd chosen *that interrogative*!

The bird stared at Tom, his beak bobbing from side-to-side, like a tutting budgerigar.

"I'm Merlin, of course! When needs-be, I can shape-shift. Crows are an intelligent and very helpful Bird-Tribe," he explained.

"Thank you, Merlin, for rescuing me," Tom told him gratefully. "I think you're wizard!"

Merlin was quite amused and told Tom that he was very pleased with the work he'd been doing. He told him to take care of himself and that he would see him again. "By the way," Merlin added, "when you go through the wind-tunnel at *Peyrepertuse,* remember to hold on to the rope."

Megan was still struggling. As she tried to reach her father, she felt a tight pull on her ankles and elbows. She looked down to see a network of fine cord meshing its way around her. She tried to call out but her vocal chords were stretched taut. Her father's image was disappearing in the mist as she felt a thud and saw hummocks of thick heather and sage swiftly passing. Her upper body was rhythmically bobbing against the back of an undulating lump.

"Where are you taking me?" a strangled sound left her lips.

"No-wer 'es yer no-ws!" came the grumbling reply.

"Put me down! Let me go!" the words whistled from her throat.

"Yer'd a mind shut up! I's got me orders," the Lump replied.

Megan wanted to thump something, someone, but her arms were secured and her ankles locked together; she didn't feel like battering her own head! No, this was not the way to be thinking. She knew plenty of facts and figures but were they of any use *now*? They came to a halt and Megan slid to the ground.

"Yer can't get awar so stay putes wile a fin' me key."

There was a clinking sound deep within the Lump and an old iron keyring appeared on the end of a stalk. A rusty key was pushed into a lock which appeared from nowhere. Megan could now see that the door was flush with the ground — it was more like a hatch. The Lump lifted it open.

"Gerin, gos on, gerin! It'll be like on chute fer yer."

"I don't want to go down there. I prefer it up here! Get me out of this mesh!" she ordered.

"They'st 'll go faster es yer ar," it told her and, with that, she felt a push and was on her way.

She flew down the narrow tunnel like a cannonball and landed in soft sand.

"Well, well, well!" were the words that greeted her.

At least they're English, Megan thought, making positivity a priority.

"Cum'st 'ere cum'st 'ere!" came the coaxing words.

"I would if I could walk properly. Can you *please* take this mesh off me!"

There was a shuffling sound and a rather large, mole-like creature came over to inspect her.

"I sees yer's been trounced!" came the verdict in a motherly sort of way.

"Don't you mean trussed?" Megan began. Then she added, "Maybe I've been trussed *and* trounced!"

Mrs Mole began to laugh. She rocked from side to side and shuffled off to fetch a useful tool. When she returned, she began an incessant *snip, snip, snip*. Megan saw that she was quite dexterously using a pair of nail clippers. It seemed like an eternity but she was finally freed. Megan looked up into Mrs Mole's face before she got to her feet. The brush of thick, grey hair around her deep-set eyes opened up to reveal black pools of pure kindness.

"We'n goin' a 'elp yer," Mrs Mole confided. "So yer's not ter mither."

Megan wondered if it was English after all but she remembered her manners. She hadn't ever realised before just how important manners could be.

"Thank you," she said simply.

"We'n dug a tunney fer yer. We'n no-wn fer ever yer'n been cumin'."

"Where does it lead to, this tunney?" Megan asked carefully.

"Back wer yer cum from, up ont'illock. Der yer wont sum'ter eat?" Mrs Mole asked thoughtfully.

Megan wondered what they would eat down here and decided against it. "No, thank you," she replied. "Can you show me where the tunney is now?"

"Yer con cum wi me, I's 'll tak yer."

So Megan followed Mrs Mole.

There was a beautifully sculpted horizontal tunnel, perhaps a metre wide. Strategically placed wooden branches, smoothed and trimmed, provided firm stepping points for Megan's trainers. Every few metres, a sconce flared in the weak current of air. Some while later they came to the end. Mrs Mole pointed upwards and Megan twisted her head to look. She was glad she'd had some climbing practice.

"A sharnt ger wi yer but yen be areet, wer'nt yer?" Mrs Mole asked.

"Yes thank you. I don't know *how* to thank you!" Megan became a bit teary.

"Yern no need. Yern free now."

Megan climbed the near-vertical tunnel, securing hand and foot-holds that had been near-perfectly placed. When she reached the top, there was a loose lid that just needed to be pushed. She heaved herself over the edge to be warmly met by Tom and Lily. They pulled her into the circle where she joined the chant.

Jean-Paul, quickly followed by Steve, stumbled onto the top of the hillock. Without making a sound, they rushed towards the others to enlarge the group and centred themselves around the fire that was still smouldering. They were all chanting now; the sound had a deeper cadence. *It was like the chanting of monks in the abbey church,* Lily thought. They began to move in a clockwise direction, stopping and alternating, clockwise and *widdershins.* The sound was hypnotic and the movement became a dance.

How much time had passed before they realised the extraordinary changes their actions had wrought, they did not know. It was Tom, his gaze moving towards the horizon, who first saw the astonishing sight. There were hundreds, perhaps thousands, of men on horseback, standards with white flags flying in the breeze, slashed with flashes of red and the glinting of metal in the sunlight. In the foreground were men and women dressed in black and blue robes, wandering through the valley and mingling with the country folk going about their daily business.

"LOOK!" Tom shouted, pointing towards the vision. "Out there! Who are they?" he gasped.

Everyone turned to see.

There was no sign of what had gone before. All seemed ordered, triumphant.

The sound of hooves coming from the distance reached them and there was a parting of the crowd.

Within minutes, a huge man on a dappled grey horse and dressed in full regalia drew close. The children recognised him immediately. He controlled his fine steed and came to a halt just before them. The Templar Knight, for that was who he was, dismounted and climbed the hill.

He knelt before them. "*Gui de Prudence*, at your service," he introduced himself. He stood and, towering above them, continued, "I cannot tell you how thankful we all are, that you have shown such valour and commitment to our cause. Through your actions and intent, we have been set free."

They each shook his hand and Jean-Paul spoke for them all.

"We are honoured to meet you and glad that we've all come through this day's trials."

Gui felt inside his cape and brought out a small casket. He opened it and asked each person to take a gift. It contained brooches made of pink coral, exquisitely carved in the shape of a rose.

"Wear this emblem and remember us — for we will never forget you. We have gathered here to show you the vastness of your work. It is now time for us to leave. God Bless you in all things."

Lily stepped forward and hugged the knight.

"Thank you for coming here today. I'm so glad we've been able to see you again."

Megan reached for his hand. He took it and held it for a long moment, remembering something as he looked into her eyes. He wanted to speak but felt that she was too young to possibly know. Yet she smiled with an openness that touched the depths of him.

He stepped back and lifted his hand in acknowledgement to the gathering clan, mounted his horse and rejoined his men without looking back.

The whole scene seemed to disappear in a light mist as they gathered their belongings to journey to their final destination.

Peyrepertuse

22

Peyrepertuse

By late afternoon, the family were making their way back towards home. The *Château of Peyrepertuse*, one of the *five sons of Carcassonne,* sat on top of a crest in the *Corbières*. It stood about six kilometres due north of their village at a height of eight hundred metres. Everyone was feeling more relaxed and satisfied that they had each achieved something worthwhile. Now there was just one more site to visit.

From the eleventh to the twelfth centuries, this castle was associated with the Counts of Barcelona and Narbonne. *Guilhem de Peyrepertuse* handed the castle over to the Seneschal of *Carcassonne* in 1240. It was fortified two years later to protect the area from Spanish attacks.

Jean-Paul drove along the narrow road through *Duilhac-sous-Peyrepertuse,* which was perched on the side of the hill that led to the castle. They pulled up by the twelfth century church, *l'Église Saint-Michel*. Laura wanted a look around here before going any further. They all got out and stretched their legs.

Steve opened the heavy wooden door and they all stepped inside. There was a hushed stillness as they walked down the central aisle towards the altar.

Bella and Lily lit candles and Laura and Megan stepped into a pew. Steve, Jean-Paul and Tom were looking at the stained-glass and memorials engraved in stone.

Daylight shone through a circular window above the altar. The rays of light fanned outwards to encompass the whole family and the carved eagle that formed the lectern. Bella walked towards it to see where the Bible was opened.

She saw that it was *Revelations, Chapter twenty-one,* and she read aloud verses one to four:

1.   Then I saw a new heaven and a new earth. The first heaven and the first earth disappeared, and the sea vanished.
2.   And I saw the Holy City, the new Jerusalem, coming down out of heaven from God, prepared and ready, like a bride dressed to meet her husband.
3.   I heard a loud voice speaking from the throne: "Now God's home is with mankind!   He will live with them, and they shall be his people. God himself will be with them, and he   will   be their God.
4.   He will wipe away all tears from their eyes. There will be no more death, no more grief or crying or pain. The old things have disappeared."

They all said *Amen* and Bella gave thanks for their safe passage and for the living prophecy that was recorded here.

The group left the church deep in thought. Jean-Paul drove them up to the castle where they parked and bought entrance tickets. It was turning six o'clock and the lady at the kiosk told them that it was a two-hour round trip. It was quite a walk to the entrance but not as daunting as their earlier ascent. Tom went running ahead, swiftly followed by Megan. Steve was wondering if they had left it too late but they had been meant to go into the church to find the prophecy.

The actual site comprised not one but two castles: *Peyrepertuse* on the east and the higher St George on the west. The ridge was three hundred metres at its longest point.

Tom was still running and Megan was catching him up. He didn't know that it was incredibly high and exposed and, where the two castles met, there was the St-Louis staircase which was dangerous in high winds.

Tom found himself breathless and faced with a steep, narrow, stone stairway leading to...well, he didn't know where! He'd no idea where Megan had got to either. The wind, that he had thought was due to his speed, was now blowing a gale. It was like being in a wind tunnel and he tried to hold on as he climbed higher. He hoped he wouldn't take off like a paper bag, twirling and whirling through the air and landing on the top of some tree.

He became quite fearful and wondered if he could turn around but he was caught in a maelstrom. He couldn't keep his eyes open for long enough to get his bearings. Then he remembered what Merlin had told him and reached down to feel the rough-hewn rock. There, securely anchored, was a thick rope. He felt his way along and reached the safety of St George's.

Megan was in the wind tunnel. She called to Tom and then realised he must have gone on ahead. It was incredibly blowy so she leaned into the wall to catch her breath. And it was here that Megan sank down to her knees and sobbed into the howling wind.

The family gathered on a craggy outcrop, east of the castle. It was the site of a chapel from where there was a superb panoramic view, taking in the *Verdouble v*alley, the *Château of Quéribus* and the Mediterranean in the distance. The whole landscape was verdant and rolling. It was an appropriate place to give thanks for the beauty of the earth and for their deliverance.

The children scanned the ancient stone wall for a suitable niche to position their crystals. They had decided, that morning, that this would be the final site for them to relinquish their own smooth stones. The rose quartz, aventurine and amber were now imbued with the most potent magical energies. They had helped to keep the children safe, had given them courage and brought into being a pathway to other dimensions. The stones belonged together.

Megan took possession of the three treasures and climbed onto Tom's shoulders. She steadied herself against the uneven rock face and stretched tall, placing them, hidden from view, into a womb-like crevice. Here they would gestate, receiving the Autumn Equinox boost and radiate their powerful energies that would activate untold transformation.

And now, with all the family members safely back together, they realised the sacred triangle was complete. They walked contentedly back to the minibus, weary but relieved.

It seemed that everyone wanted to shower or bathe and to change into something cosy. It was agreed that a lie-in was *de rigueur* the following morning and any further organisation could wait until then.

The children ran upstairs to do their own thing. Tom was keen to tell his sisters about Merlin the Crow! Megan wanted to give them an account of her Great Escape and Lily felt that she had shown great stamina and courage, getting to the top of *Montségur.*

Jean-Paul opened a bottle of champagne. He and Bella had had the most rewarding summer holiday of their lives and most of it was due to the children.

Bella proposed a toast, "To the family; long may it support, nurture and grow!"

Steve added, "To health, happiness and the Work!"

They sat listening to Debussy's *La Mer,* chatting and enjoying an ambient evening with people they knew so well.

23

A Weekend to Remember

The next day brought a flurry of activity. Everyone had things to do. Bella wanted to bake and freeze Tom's birthday cake. Megan and Lily still had work to do on their brother's presents. Jean-Paul and Steve decided to clean out the minibus and Laura tidied up the house and her children's clothes. She helped them pack for their overnight stay, choosing items that she thought would be suitable to wear when meeting the Pope, though most of their wardrobe was casual.

Jean-Paul prepared a mixed salad for lunch and Lily made a special dressing. Steve and Tom set the table on the terrace.

"What time are we setting off?" Tom asked between mouthfuls of crunchy, homemade coleslaw. It was sweet with pieces of apple amongst the grated carrot, sultanas and white cabbage.

"Shall we leave at about half past two?" Bella suggested.

"That sounds good. Then we've got time to look around the village before dinner," Jean-Paul agreed.

They all had fresh fruit from the garden before clearing away.

Lily was thrilled that her parents would get to see *St Guilhem;* she wanted to show them the Abbey Church and the lovely river running behind the hotel. Megan wanted them to stand on Devil's Bridge with the spectacular view of the *Hérault* Gorge, where they had come through in their kayaks.

All their bags were put into the back of the minibus. Then Jean-Paul and Steve closed the shutters and locked up the house, checking to see that they had left nothing behind. Steve studied the map and Jean-Paul drove once more. The children settled themselves in the back. It was going to take a couple of hours, traffic permitting.

Megan was reading a leaflet on the Pope's Palace at Avignon and occasionally giving the others snippets of information.

"The construction began in 1335 and it took just under twenty years to complete. It's the largest Gothic Palace in Europe," she told them.

"The position of the palace is superb," Bella said. "It overlooks the city and the Rhone river. The Avignon Theatre performs in the open air in the Honour Courtyard every year in July."

"Which part of the palace will we be going to?" asked Tom.

"It will be the Pope's Private Chambers," Bella told him.

"Are you looking forward to meeting the Pope?" Laura asked her children.

"Oh, yes!" said Lily emphatically. "He looks a very kind man when I've seen him on the telly. I wonder what he'll ask us?"

"We've just got to be ourselves," Megan replied. "I should think he'll want to know something about the amazing things that have happened to us over the holidays."

"Just see what comes to mind at the time," Steve told them. "You don't need to prepare anything. Let it be natural and spontaneous."

"I'm sure he simply wants to meet the friendly and interesting children that you are," Laura reassured them.

"I can't wait to see Michel," Lily said. "What time is he meeting us?"

"At seven o'clock in the foyer, then it's dinner at half past," their mother told them.

"I'm looking forward to seeing *St Guilhem*, after everything you've told us," Steve turned to his children.

"You'll definitely think it's great, Dad," Megan smiled.

They were heading towards *Béziers*. Jean-Paul thought that Steve and Laura would like to call at *Pézenas*. Then it would be another thirty kilometres or so to their destination.

"*Pézenas* is a lovely town. It's very lively at this time of year with folk festivals, concerts and craft fairs. If we're lucky, Tom, we may get to hear some live music," Jean-Paul told him.

"*Molière* visited *Pézenas* in the seventeenth century and put on some plays and farces in the covered square," Bella told them. She was keen on the theatre and often took her students to see classical plays.

A little while later, they arrived at the small town and managed to find a parking space. There was a great atmosphere, with throngs of people wandering along the pavements amongst antique shops and stylish buildings with wrought iron balconies, housing gift shops and artisans' workshops. Many of its mansions hadn't changed since the seventeenth century.

As they turned a corner a square opened out, surrounded by several cafés. A folk band was entertaining the visitors and locals alike.

"This music's from the Celtic tradition," Jean-Paul commented. "How do you like it, Tom?"

"It's good! I like the Celtic rhythms," he said, mimicking *River Dance*!

"Let's sit here," Laura suggested. "I think we've got some Celtic blood in us," she said laughingly to Bella.

The trio consisted of an accordion-player, a fiddler and a flautist. The audience clapped when they finished the next tune. Then the fiddler asked if anyone would like to join them. It seemed that there should have been a fourth member. Steve and Laura were surprised when Tom nodded and stood up. He was handed a violin.

The three set up a gentle rhythm and the accordion-player counted him in. Tom began to play an improvisation. The crowd became silent, spellbound! Feet and hands were keeping time. Eventually, he brought the tune to a close. The band members were stunned and patted him on the back. The onlookers clapped and cheered, shouting *Bravo*! *Encore*! There was talk of an opening for Tom if he decided to stay in France!

All too soon it was time to continue on to *St Guilhem.* As they drew nearer to the village, Steve commented on how isolated it was, with outcrops of granite and access only by the Devil's Bridge. Jean-Paul pulled over so that they could walk across it. Megan's parents were impressed with the savage beauty of the craggy gorge, steeply rising, through which swirled the River *Hérault,* breaking into rapids as it flooded over the rocks.

"However did you kayak through here?" Laura asked.

"It wasn't so swollen when *we* came through," Tom told them.

"And Uncle Jean-Paul went through first so that we could follow," Megan added. "Sometimes you have to rise to the challenge, Mum. It really was great fun!"

Tom and Megan took some photos of the family and the views and Laura thought how right Megan was. She was growing, becoming more confident and independent. No doubt there would be many more challenges to come.

They returned to the car for the short drive to the hotel. Jean-Paul had booked them into *Le Guilhaume d'Orange* once again. Laura and Steve were delighted with the setting and eager to look around the village. After leaving the luggage in their rooms, they set off up the steep, narrow street towards the square and the shade of the great plane tree.

After a refreshing shower and changing into something dressier for dinner, the whole family arrived in the foyer where Michel was waiting. It was unbelievable that they had first met him only a few weeks before; they were all so comfortable in each other's company and there was a strong chord of trust and friendship. How many people could one trust implicitly? How many people had the awareness and integrity to simply want the best for you? And to know what *was* the best? Their relationship had a whole new dimension.

The waiter ushered them through to a large, welcoming table.

"Merlin would be thrilled to be here," Michel told them. "He is only a thought away."

"Give Merlin our best wishes and tell him that we are grateful for all his help," Steve told Michel.

He was struck by the knowledge that their relationship would last throughout their lives — and possibly beyond.

"Merlin helped me into the circle at *Montségur*," Tom told Michel. "I didn't know that he could change himself into a crow!"

"Merlin uses magic in many ways. He is able to manifest that which dwells in the void. I have been his apprentice for many years and many lifetimes and yet I still have much to learn."

"What will the Pope want to know?" Lily asked Michel, getting down to business.

"He is very interested in your experiences here in France. Age and status do not have a monopoly on experience and wisdom. The Pope is a seeker of the Truth, which is often found in innocence and openness. Many people, as they grow older, become more mistrustful of life. They are not open to its magic and freshness. Just be yourselves tomorrow. It will be a friendly and very informal meeting. I shall introduce you and remain throughout. Merlin has given me something for the Pope. I wonder if you would like to hand it over to him, Lily?"

"Yes, I'd love to, Michel. What is it?"

Michel opened his briefcase and placed on the table an old wooden box. It reminded Lily of the one the monk had shown them the last time they were here. She picked it up and, flanked by Megan and Tom, opened it. Inside was a golden amulet on an antique chain. Their eyes widened.

"For the Pope?" they all asked in surprise.

Tom thought that the Pope would already be wearing symbolic jewellery, handed down through generations of popes, which represented the Catholic Church and Faith.

Megan asked the key question, "Will the Pope wear it?"

"We shall find out tomorrow," Michel replied.

They ordered aperitifs and chose a three-course meal from the short, yet appetising, menu. There was a great atmosphere as they shared their experiences of the past week. Michel had a good sense of humour as well as showing great sensitivity to their challenges. By nine-thirty they were all feeling pleasantly full, relaxed and ready for bed. They agreed to meet Michel in the morning, at nine o'clock, for the drive to Avignon.

Their first view of the Pope's Palace was breathtaking, even compared to the castles they had visited. This was on another scale, with imposing walls flanked by four enormous towers. Aunt Bella was right; the setting by the river was beautiful.

"That's the Saint Benezet Bridge; the one from the song, *"Sur le Pont d'Avignon,"* Bella told them.

The children couldn't resist giving their rendition in the back of the car.

"Michel gave me a parking pass so we can go through like royalty," Steve told them.

Laura was glad that they hadn't got to find parking and then walk to their destination. She was beginning to feel a bit nervous.

"There's over fifteen thousand square metres of floor space," Megan told them, "and visitors can see over twenty rooms."

"The Great Chapel houses an art exhibition every summer. This year its theme is *Pont*," Bella told the children. "Perhaps you'd like to see that later?"

"I'd love that!" Lily said.

"We'll do that, then, and Megan and Tom can choose what they'd like to do," Laura said, balancing things out.

"We'd like to go on the river," Tom said, without having to think, and Megan agreed.

Michel led the way to the Pope's Private Chambers. The children were awed to be in such a historically significant place. The adults tried to remain casual and relaxed about the meeting.

When Michel pressed a button, a large wooden door opened and they were all invited inside. The Pope was actually there to meet them.

"I'm so pleased that you could come," he said, moving forward to greet them. He invited them to sit down and requested refreshments for his guests. The Pope's assistant brought these in, accompanied by a very well-behaved, chocolate-coloured Labradoodle who introduced himself to the children first of all.

They answered the Pope's questions thoughtfully and honestly: *What had they enjoyed about their stay in France? What had they found most interesting? Had any particular experience opened their minds to new things?*

Megan, Tom and Lily enjoyed this opportunity to recount things that were important to them as individuals. There was no sense of hurry or that His Grace was anything other than deeply interested in each of them and their perspective on life. Occasionally, he asked their parents and aunt and uncle something to find out their views. Finally, the Pope asked if they would share a short prayer time with him.

At this point, Bella took out the Rosary and briefly explained how it came to be in her possession. His Grace was visibly moved and asked if he could hold it.

"Bella, this Rosary has deep significance for the Catholic Faith. Do you know of *Saint Dominic*? The Sacred Rosary of Mary lies at the heart of the Dominican Order."

"When did he live, Your Grace?" she asked with a keenness of interest.

"Saint Dominic was born in Spain in 1170. Towards the end of 1204, he came to Rome to visit Pope Innocent III and was sent to the *Languedoc.* He based himself at the Church of *Notre Dame de Prouille,* to the west of *Carcassonne.* He set about helping to convert the Cathars and, in his lifetime, travelled widely and helped many.

"One day, he was praying in his church, asking for assistance with the task that lay ahead. By some miracle of Grace, the Blessed Virgin Mary appeared to him and gave him the Holy Rosary."

"What year was that, Your Grace?" Bella asked.

"It was in the year 1208. Some historians say that he was on the streets of *Béziers,* trying to help people on that first day of the Albigensian War, the 22nd July, 1209."

Bella was stunned. She felt the need to share her insight with her family and the Pope. "It was Saint Dominic who handed me this Sacred Rosary; I know it." She recounted their meeting with a sense of awe and gratitude.

A few minutes of silence passed as each person registered this astounding information — they were in possession of the very same Rosary that had come from Mother Mary herself! The children had not only met her, the family had been given a sacred gift imbued with her own powerful and compassionate healing energies! The gift was a priceless treasure and a physical reminder of the miraculous events they had all experienced.

The Pope led prayers of thanksgiving. Afterwards, he asked Bella if he could borrow the Rosary for prayers at the Vatican. He told her that Michel would return it safely at the right time. The Pope thanked them for their commitment, courage and honesty. Lily stepped forward to present His Holiness with the gift. He received it graciously.

217

"Would you do me the honour of placing this emblem of Truth over my gown, Michel?"

When it was in place, he motioned for everyone to sit down for a few moments.

"We are no doubt living in very special times. The things that you have so willingly and honestly shared with me today have opened my heart and touched my soul. The boundaries between groups and belief systems are dissolving because they are man-made. God cannot be contained. His path is inclusive not exclusive. It is time to reveal hidden information. People need to know the Truth so that they may grow and understand their place in this vast Universe. You are all blessed and, through you and others like you, God's Word will become manifest on Earth. Thank you for coming to meet me and God bless you now and always."

Lily dabbed her eyes when it was time to leave and Tom felt like he did on the last day of term, a sense of completion and excitement yet, somehow, also loss.

Michel led the way outside. After thanking them for their company and friendship, he told them that he would be in touch.

24

Tom's Birthday Challenge

It was Tom's twelfth birthday and he was awake early to open his presents. Megan had made a montage of photographs to put up in his school dormitory. Lily gave him a painting of *St Guilhem-le-Désert*, which held wonderful memories of their holiday. Steve and Laura had bought him some clothes and a generous voucher from Amazon so that he could download any new music he wanted to listen to. Bella and Jean-Paul gave Tom a bird book, a pair of binoculars and a book of Celtic violin music. Since Merlin's timely landing, he had become fascinated by bird species! There was a chocolate cake waiting for later, his favourite. Tom was well pleased!

Steve asked Tom what he wanted to do on his special day. They hadn't been up into the Pyrenees yet, and they were going home in the morning, so he asked if everyone else would like to go. It was a resounding yes. Bella reminded them to take some warmer clothes because the mountains had their own micro-climate. Jean-Paul asked if they would like to have lunch at a good restaurant he knew in a mountain town called *Prats-de-Mollo-la-Preste* in the

Haut Vallespir. It sounded like a good idea, so he made a reservation.

After a quick tidy round, they went upstairs to sort out suitable clothes and footwear. Steve and Jean-Paul studied the map; it was a bit of a tortuous journey which was inevitable on mountain roads. They would be heading towards and around the *Pic du Canigou* and then onto the D115 which ran south-westwards to *Prats.*

They set off at eleven, hoping to reach the town by about one.

"*Prats-de-Mollo* is a strategically positioned town," Jean-Paul told them. "Its fortifications were designed by *Vauban*, the French military engineer, to keep the border safe from Aragon, a region in north-east Spain."

"That's really surprising!" Tom commented. "I know the castles were fortified but I didn't expect to see a *walled town* in the mountains."

"*Vauban* seems to have left his mark everywhere," Steve said.

"The locals speak Catalan so, even if you know French and Spanish, it can sometimes be difficult to communicate. Further to the south-east is a village called *Coustouges.* It lies on an escape route that Spanish Republicans took, fleeing General Franco during the Spanish Civil War in the 1930's. The people were destitute and took the arduous mountain pass to find freedom and safety," Jean-Paul explained.

"If there's time," Bella said, "we could have a look at the village. Otherwise, we'll leave it for another holiday. On Mid-Summer's Eve, the French and Spanish Catalonians meet on Mount *Canigou* to light the first of their bonfires and use torches lit from this to spread beacons throughout the region.

It's an all-night vigil that ends at sunrise. Then they collect wild flowers, like vervain and St John's Wort, which are made into crosses to hang on their doors for protection," Bella explained.

"So, you weren't the only ones picking wild flowers at that time of year!" Laura told her children.

As they were driving through *Arles-sur-Tech*, Bella asked Jean-Paul if he could park up because she wanted to show the family something of interest. The town had grown up around an abbey built on the banks of the River Tech in 900AD. Most of this had disappeared but a twelfth century abbey church stood firm. Bella pointed to a fourth century, white-marble sarcophagus to the left of the main door.

"This is the *Sainte-Tombe*. Every year, several hundred litres of pure, clear water seep from it. There has been no scientific explanation," Bella said, looking rather mystified.

The children were intrigued.

"The Holy Tomb is in a sheltered place so it can't be anything to do with rainfall," Megan said.

"That's true," Bella nodded.

"Marble isn't porous, is it?" Tom asked.

"Yes it is, Tom," Steve said. "But it's polished to be incredibly hard and durable, which is why it's used for things like flooring, statues and headstones."

"What happens to the water that comes from this tomb?" Lily asked her aunt.

"I don't know. Maybe it's used for baptisms and such like. It has obviously been tested and there are no traces of impurities."

"Maybe it has magical properties," Megan suggested.

It was a mystery — and the children liked a mystery!

Prats-de-Mollo-la-Preste was a lively Catalan town in the peaceful setting of the upper Tech Valley. They could see a huge Gothic-style church and there were the remains of a seventeenth century fortress. After parking, they walked up to the Belleview Hotel, just in time for lunch in the restaurant. Steve proposed a toast to Tom and they sang *Happy Birthday.*

After wandering around the village in the late-summer sunshine, they decided to drive a little further and then walk through part of the nearby *Forêt Dominiale du Haut Vallespir.*

It was a good opportunity for Tom to use his new binoculars so he slung them over his head as they parked just off the roadside. Tom got out and looked up into the clear skies, sheltering his eyes from the bright sunlight. He heard several high-pitched calls and saw, first one, then a second and a third huge bird appear over a crest, soaring and riding the thermals. He trained his binoculars on these awesome birds and identified them as bearded vultures.

"You have earned yourself ten points, Tom, or should that be thirty?" Jean-Paul asked him jokingly.

"Let me see, quick, let me see Tom!" Lily made a grab for the binoculars.

Megan was rummaging in Tom's rucksack to find his bird book. "I'm just going to look those up and then can I see before they disappear?"

There was a queue. Megan confirmed that Tom had identified the bearded vultures correctly. Everyone peered at these wild, yet amenable birds. Then Tom scanned the countryside for any other interesting features. He could identify Fort *Lagarde*, built on a rocky outcrop, with higher peaks behind. Sheep were grazing in the high pastures for the summer months; wheat, rye and maize were ripening and, as he circled round, the majestic *Pic du Canigou* came into view. It rose to nearly two thousand eight hundred metres and was snow-capped for most of the year.

Laura thought they should hurry if they were to enjoy a walk before the journey home so they set off determinedly into the shady forest. The children went first, having decided to be as quiet as possible to avoid disturbing the wildlife. No fits of laughter, no screams if someone happened to trip over.

Matronly chestnut trees laden with ripening fruits stood open-armed. *A fortnight later*, thought Tom, *and I could have the biggest conkers in the school!* Sturdy beech trees lined the trail, their delicate leaves fluttering in the currents of air and towering Scots pine pushed their dark green, shaggy heads towards the sky. The rustling of birds and tiny creatures in the undergrowth stilled as they walked by. It was very difficult to spot wild animals in their natural habitat.

Jean-Paul noticed some marks on a nearby holm oak, about a metre and a half above the ground. He motioned for the others to take a closer look. There were two sets of deeply-gouged marks, running almost horizontally. Bella, Laura and Steve looked questioningly at Jean-Paul.
"What could have made those?" Steve asked.
"It could only be one thing..." Jean-Paul replied in a quiet voice, "... a brown bear."
"Let's look for footprints," Laura suggested. "Have you ever done any tracking, Jean-Paul?"
"Yes, I've been on a few wild boar hunts in the past. It's a bit nerve–racking. Wild boar can be quite vicious when cornered."

"And what about brown bears?" Bella asked him nervously.

"There may well be tracks if we look carefully."

Laura took in a great gasp of air, "Where are the children?"

Everyone looked up and around — and then at each other. They were nowhere to be seen.

"M...E...GAAA...NN!   T...O...O...O...M! LI...LLLYYYY!!!" Laura shouted between cupped hands into the vacant air.

Jean-Paul immediately put both hands onto her shoulders and pulled her towards him to gain her full attention.

"Laura, we need to be quiet, calm. We don't want to startle the animal."

"Are brown bears dangerous?" she asked him urgently.

"Only when cornered, if they've got youngsters...or...if they're hungry!"

He wished he'd said nothing; Laura looked as if she were about to cry.

"Look, the important thing now is to find the children!" Steve said emphatically.

"Those marks could have been made days or weeks ago!"

"You're right," agreed Jean-Paul. "Let's split up into two groups, keep to the marked paths and move quickly. We can stay in touch by mobile. Let's just try those out. The children can't have gone far." The thing was that Jean-Paul had noticed what he thought were bear tracks earlier and there were fresh droppings nearby. He said nothing more, but thought they could be in trouble, big trouble!

Steve and Laura set off along the left fork in the path. Jean-Paul and Bella carried on, moving quickly and quietly. They resisted the urge to shout the children's names so as not to startle anything that might be wild and dangerous.

Tom, Megan and Lily had gone off the designated path and deeper into the forest. Tom had spotted a red squirrel weaving its way through the branches and jumping acrobatically from tree to tree so they had followed as surreptitiously as they could manage.

They heard a few different birdsong and something making very noisy, insistent squeaks as if calling a warning. Tom glanced across to his left, thinking that he had seen a movement. Yes, something *was* moving. He stopped and put his finger up to his lips, pointing in the direction of a beige-coloured shape peering out from behind a beech tree. It looked as if it could be standing on hind legs. They instinctively crouched down, on the one hand thinking of hiding, and not disturbing the visitor on the other.

Laura was becoming frantic. They were running along the path, hidden beneath the oppressive trees. The once beautiful woodland was taking on the appearance of something more sinister and dangerous. Where were they? The children?

"We should be shouting, calling their names! They're getting further and further away from us! We don't even know that we're going in the right direction! They should have been given mobile phones for their birthdays! How foolish we are to be worried about brain tumours when they could be eaten by bears!"

"Laura! Stop it! We'll find them...they couldn't have gone far! The four of us are on the paths they would have taken. Let's phone J.P."

Megan whispered in Tom's ear, "It's a bear, a brown bear!"

They were stunned.

"Don't make a sound," Tom told his sisters between gritted teeth.

"What do they like to eat?" Lily whispered.

Tom resisted the temptation to say *little girls* and thought carefully about what would *not* upset Lily. "Wild fruits at this time of year, I should think," he replied quietly.

"I've seen some forest fruits," she said happily. "I'll go and collect them — wild raspberries and bilberries."

Tom did not want anyone to move, to attract any more attention, but it was too late. Lily crawled off in the direction they had come from.

The bear seemed to be watching them. What should they do? They couldn't go anywhere or Lily would be lost. Come to think of it, they were already lost! Tom was feeling a bit hot and sweaty; he undid the button of his polo shirt and found his pendant hanging from a piece of leather. He took hold of it and looked up at Megan. She nodded, knowing that they needed help.

"Help us, Merlin, help us!" he pleaded.

Jean-Paul was tracking, using all his skills and senses. He and Bella were moving stealthily from one clue to the next: broken grasses, fresh droppings, flattened patches of moss and the occasional paw print where the earth was damp. They were on to him and he was moving fast! And Jean-Paul was aware of avoiding their scent drifting downwind.

Lily came crawling back with her snack-box half filled with delicious-looking berries.

"He'll love these," she said as if they were taking part in a pantomime and two children under a bear costume were about to make their entrance.

Megan told her to shush.

The bear was on all fours now and bounding towards them! Tom held the pendant tight and, praying, threw himself in front of the girls. As it reached Tom, it slowed and once more raised itself up onto hind legs. Lily, fearless, stood up and held out her snack- box. The bear's nostrils flared; he stuck his nose into the box and snuffled his way through the berries until it was quite empty.

They all stood up, facing the bear. It seemed to speak.

"Well done, Tom! You were very brave. You would risk your own life to protect your sisters. And well done, Megan, for keeping a cool head, identifying the potential enemy and thinking of the safety of you all. But very well done Lily! You remained your true Self and showed great kindness to a fellow creature. No thought of fear or danger entered your head and, for *this* reason, you are all safe. Enjoy the rest of your special day, Tom. Thank you, once again, for your kindness."

With that, the magnificent bear loped off through the forest. There was something of Merlin about the whole episode. All three children were deep in thought, absorbing the unexpected message and the lesson that they had learned from their younger sister. They dusted themselves down and, just as they were deciding which way to go, they saw Aunt Bella and Uncle Jean-Paul coming into view. It was a very relieved set of adults who escorted them back to the car. The children seemed oblivious to the danger they had been in and their parents preferred it this way. There was no more trauma to recover from...was there?

The journey home didn't seem to take as long as the outward one; the roads were a little less tortuous. When they arrived, they had showers and got changed so that they could sort out their belongings for packing. It was rather sad, the end of the holidays and having to say goodbye to their aunt and uncle. It didn't bear thinking about.

When everything was sorted and the minibus packed, they settled round the oak table for one last evening meal together.

"It's a good thing it's your birthday today, Tom," Bella told him. "Otherwise, it would be a very sad day." She put her arms around him. "So, after a wonderful day outdoors, let's continue the celebrations!"

Jean-Paul had made fresh pizzas and a salad. Bella had decorated a chocolate gateau with candles and three edible birds. Steve was opening a bottle of champagne for the occasion whilst the children enjoyed their favourite *Oranginas*.

25

New Beginnings

The household woke early. The Worthington family were catching the ten o'clock flight and needed to be at the airport an hour earlier. Before leaving, they checked all through the house for stray belongings, then they all settled into the minibus, seemingly with far more luggage than they had come with. Bella was feeling...well, she was feeling a bit strange. When she got out of bed this morning she had felt distinctly queasy. Was she coming down with something?

Jean-Paul was rather thoughtful as he drove the family to the airport. He would miss the children immensely. It was great that he worked with youngsters but it wasn't the same as having family living with you. Things were going to be a whole lot quieter from now on.

Megan's mind was already thinking of the new school that she would be starting, of going to buy her uniform and making new friends. Tom was glad that he would be spending time with his mates from school and looking out for his kid-sister, who had risen beyond measure in his esteem! Lily was thinking of new everythings.

They arrived at *Rivesaltes*, parked up, and helped with the luggage into Departures. There wasn't a long queue so it only took a few minutes to check in. There were lots of hugs, kisses and tears. They all knew that they would keep in touch but they found themselves promising this. The children had thoughtful gifts to give to their Aunt Bella and Uncle Jean-Paul so they handed them over and told them they were not to be opened until they got home. They waved to each other as Bella and her husband walked back to their car.

As they set off, Bella felt Jean-Paul's sadness as well as her own but something totally unexpected occurred to her.

"Jean-Paul, can we call at the *Pharmacie* on our way home?" she asked.

"Yes, of course. What's the matter? Aren't you feeling very well? I thought you looked a bit peeky this morning. You know, Bella, you're bound to be a bit upset. I know *I* am. I think you should have a rest when we get in; you've done so much this summer holiday."

He was about to say something else so she blurted out to cut him off, "Jean-Paul, stop the car as soon as you can!"

"You're not going to be sick, are you?" he asked with a look of horror.

"No, but you might faint when I tell you what I *want* to tell you!" she said with feeling.

Jean-Paul pulled up safely, if a little suddenly. "What is it Bella?"

"I think I'm...we're...going to have a baby!" she spluttered and burst into tears.

Jean-Paul started to cry too. They sat in the car for a while, gazing into each others' eyes and sobbing — tears of absolute joy.

When they finally pulled themselves together, they continued their journey home. Bella's mind went back to her meeting with Mother Mary and to the evening when Laura had told her that she, too, was blessed.

Lily, Tom and Megan boarded the plane with their parents in tow. Lily was looking for the first free row; she wanted a window seat. She left her rucksack on the aisle seat for Megan to stow away and settled in, fastening her safety belt. Tom sat beside her and, within a few minutes, the engines were revving, ready for take-off.

As the plane began to gain height, Lily could see the receding French countryside that she so loved. *I shall never forget this holiday*, she thought. She turned to Tom and Megan. "Do you think we will ever see Michel and Merlin again?"

"I'm sure we will," Tom replied and Megan added knowingly, "Life is a beautiful mystery that unfolds in its *own* time."

Afterword

Autumn Equinox

If any human beings had found themselves hovering on the summit of a castle in south-west France on this particular morning — they would have been vaporised. Cells of matter transmuted into light, outer senses rendered redundant, intelligent awareness transported through the ether into the soul of origin and strands of DNA transferred to life beyond life. With the catching of the first light, the encoded crystals received and relayed an unparalleled surge of Cosmic Power, the like of which the Earth, in all her ancient and wise history, had never before experienced.

This was just the beginning…
of the Ascension Prophecy!

Glossary

p1	*Bonjour, ça va?*	Hello, how are you?
p2	*le coq-au-vin*	chicken and red wine casserole
	le magret du canard	duck breast
	à la pâte	with pasta
	les moules-frites	mussels and chips
	une omelette au fromage	cheese omelette
p3	*Pyrénées-Orientales*	Eastern Pyrenees
p4	*les habitants*	village dwellers
p8	*JBCA*	Jodrell Bank Centre for Astrophysics
	charcuterie	slices of cold meats
p9	*solar plexus*	complex of nerves at the pit of the stomach
p21	*l'Église Notre-Dame des-Anges*	Our Lady of the Angels Church
p24	*le poulet rôti et frites*	chicken and chips
	les boules de glâces à la vanille et au chocolat	scoops of vanilla and chocolate ice-cream
	des citrons pressés	fresh lemon with water

p30	*Chemin du Fauvisme*	Fauvist Way, tourist path displaying the art style of Fauvism 1905-08
p30	*les Hospitaliers*	Order founded in 1099 - present
p30	*les Grottes des Demoiselles*	Fairy Caves
p32	*Place de la Madeleine*	Magdalene Square
	Bistrot des Halles	small market restaurant
p33	*l'Église de la Madeleine*	Mary Magdalene's Church
p36	la *Crêperie*	pancake shop, restaurant
p46	*pains au chocolat*	chocolate buns
p48	*travail*	work
p51	*la Librairie*	Bookshop/Stationers
p54	*une montgolfière*	an early hot-air balloon
p63	*en plein air*	outside
p74	*Bonne chance. Adieu*	Good luck. Farewell
p81	un *Kir Royale*	Champagne cocktail, with cassis
p101	*Connaître les Cathares*	Know the Cathars
p106	*la Charcuterie*	delicatessen
	une salade niçoise	salad made with tuna, eggs, anchovies etc.

p113	*verbatim*	word for word
p114	*chambre d'hôte*	Guest House
	Le Domaine de St-Jean	St. John's Estate
	La Maison sur la Colline	The House on the Hill
	Green Guide	The Michelin Green Guide
p115	*La Route des Abbayes du Languedoc - Roussillon*	The Abbeys of Languedoc-Roussillon written by Frederique Barbut
p137	*the lotus posture*	a position where both feet are resting on the thighs, for meditation
p150	*Croeso!*	Welcome! In Welsh
p153	*abettor*	one who assists in an offence
p157	*Karma*	the universal law of cause and effect
p171	*le Château Comtal*	Count's Castle
p183	*le Pays Cathare*	Tourist name for Cathar Country
	five sons of Carcassonne	Castles of Peyrepertuse, Aguilar, Termes, Quéribus and Puilaurens
p199	*widdershins*	an old word for anti-clockwise

237

Acknowledgements

I should like to thank Mary, Barbara, Judith and Lisa, members of my Meditation Group, who have believed in this book from its inception. Thank you for your constant encouragement, enthusiastic responses to my impromptu readings and total conviction that it would one day become published. My three daughters have always known that I was capable of accomplishing the task. So thank you Amelia, Laura, and Rachel for your loving support. I give special recognition to my eldest, Amelia, for being available and keen to discuss the development of the plot and for giving me several useful pointers in the early stages.

My heartfelt thanks go to Maggie Kneen, a talented children's author and illustrator, who agreed to design the amazing cover, illustrations and map that wonderfully enhance the text. We met just at the moment when I needed a sign that my manuscript was to become a real book. It was a synchronicity that we both recognised and cherished. Maggie has also proven to be an inspired editor, who has encouraged me to develop my descriptive work, with a well-placed comment, *dig deeper Ann,* or a significant question. Thank you for your warmth, honesty and integrity, Maggie, and for putting your trust in me.

In Corfu last year, I met Alex Christou, a warm-hearted eco-warrior; the perfect embodiment of my Templar Knight, *Gui de Prudence.* Alex agreed to pose for several portrait shots by our brilliant retreat photographer, Julie-lou Weston. And Maggie worked her artistic magic in capturing his essence for the front cover. Thank you all for a superb collaboration and outcome.

Recently I contacted a friend and climber, Roger Brown, to advise me on the climbing scene in Chapter 21. He was able to add the technical expertise needed to enhance the assault on *Montségur.* Thank you Roger for saving me!

Thanks go to Moyra Irving for agreeing to read my manuscript and give valuable feedback. Moyra was the perfect person: an editor, published author, and modern languages graduate. Most importantly, she has totally understood and appreciated the spiritual depth of my book and has given it an amazing review.

When I thought I had finished this novel I met the lovely Siân-Elin Flint-Freel, an incisive proof-reader and editor, who accepted my request to help finalise the text ready for publication. She has been an inspiration and a joy to work with, helping me to bring a fluency and clarity to the finest threads of the plot.

I should also like to thank Jane Noble Knight for her brilliant *Writing and Publishing a Best-Seller* course which she offers with humour, integrity and great practicality. And thanks to

John Beaumont at *Prontaprint* for typesetting this book and for his relaxed approach and expertise. At various stages in my writing I have been encouraged by Sylvia Kemp, creative writing tutor at the Congleton U3A and her lovely group, Christine McGrory, initiator of *The Key*, Jackie Murray, Alison Clewes and Debbie Hayes. Rachel Elnaugh of *Source T.V.* and Bret Shah of local radio have helped with promotional ideas, thank you. Several people have kindly agreed to read and review my book. I am grateful to Lisa Ray and Sara Knowles for their heart-warming responses.

And finally thank you to my partner, Gary, who has through necessity become a good provider of appetizing meals! Gary led me to some of the most beautiful and interesting places in France which would one day become the inspiration for my debut novel.

Ann Campbell   October, 2014.

About the Author

Ann Campbell has taught in Primary and Middle schools for over twenty years. She has studied and practised meditation, yoga and natural healing techniques throughout her adult life. Ann has always had a keen interest in the deeper questions about our existence and continues to be a seeker of the Truth.

The author lives in Cheshire, England, with her partner and has three children and five grandchildren.

Notes

Notes

Notes

Made in the USA
Charleston, SC
16 December 2014